HE'S ALIVE, BUT!

by

Mark A. Anderson

Order this book online at www.trafford.com
or email orders@trafford.com

Most Trafford titles are also available at major online book retailers.

Note for Librarians: A cataloguing record for this book is available from Library
and Archives Canada at www.collectionscanada.ca/amicus/index-e.html

Printed in Victoria, BC, Canada.

ISBN: 978-1-4269-0980-1 (sc)
ISBN: 978-1-4269-0982-5 (eBook)
ISBN: 978-1-4269-1576-5 (hc)

*Our mission is to efficiently provide the world's finest, most comprehensive book publishing
service, enabling every author to experience success. To find out how to publish your book, your
way, and have it available worldwide, visit us online at www.trafford.com*

Trafford rev. 08/04/09

 www.trafford.com

North America & international
toll-free: 1 888 232 4444 (USA & Canada)
phone: 250 383 6864 ♦ fax: 812 355 4082

DEDICATION

I dedicate this book to the

Memory of my grandmother: Mary Bednar, my father

Floyd Jay Anderson Jr. and to all the friends I lost along the way.

ACKNOWLEDGEMENTS

First and foremost I would like to acknowledge my parents; Floyd

and Catherine for showing their support and being there when I

needed them. I next would like to thank my sister Linda and

mother Catherine for their assistance with this book. My wife

Kameha, my son Mark and daughter Athena, I love you all very

much. I must not forget all of my friends and relatives for their

support and encouragement throughout. Last but not least I would

like to thank you, the reader, for if it weren't for you, there

wouldn't be any books

CHAPTER I

HE'S ALIVE, BUT!

WHEN A BABY TAKES THE VOYAGE,
DOWN THE PASSAGE OF LIFE.
THEY ARE UNAWARE OF THEIR SURROUNDINGS,
AND ARE INSECURE.
BUT WHEN THE ADULTS TAKE THE VOYAGE,
THEY ARE AWARE, YET STILL INSECURE,
SO THEY HIDE WITHIN THEMSELVES.

Friday, November 13th, 1981.

Anita Homza is lying in a hospital bed in Berwick, Pa. She just gave birth to her first son and is waiting news about her husband.

Anita thinks back to this afternoon when her husband Wayne and she were in their trailer and the phone rang sending chills down her spine. She watched the expression on his face while he was talking, then his face tightened up and she knew that someone said something to anger him. He quickly hung the phone up and took Anita next door to a neighbor's house (Gail Cooper).

Anita knows Wayne could take care of himself in any situation. When they first net, Anita was wheel chair bound. The doctors said that she'd never walk again. Then Wayne came along and touched her, and she was able to once again walk, and do the things that she was able to do while she was in the wheelchair. No, Anita knows that Wayne not only could heal with a simple thought, hut could kill with a single thought. Yet, she lays in bed worrying that something terrible has happened to her husband.

Anita is drawn from her thoughts by the opening of the door. In walks a short, brown haired woman.

"Gail, did you find Wayne yet?"

"I'm sorry Anita; I've been trying your trailer for the last six hours but no answer."

"Did you try his mother?"

"No, I don't know her number."

"Look in the address book that's in the night stand."

"I've got it, I'll go try it, be right back."

10:30 p.m. at the Nanticoke, Pa. Hospital. Tom Brinkle is waking up.

"Lay back down Mr. Brinkle, you have a slight concussion." A nurse says. Tom tries to focus at the image in front of him.

"How is Wayne?" Tom asks while holding his head.

"Mr. Homza will be alright. We have him in another room."

"Did anyone call his wife?"

"Yes, but there wasn't any answer."

"What about his mother?"

"He didn't have that number on him, do you know it?"

"If you'll get my pants, it should be in my address book." tom Brinkle is an investigative reporter for a local, television station. He was following reports of a man going around healing people. He wanted to find out if this man was for real and if he was what a great news item he would make. So he continued to search and make inquiries, which led him to Wayne Homza's house. Tom became close to Wayne and his family trying to find out more information about him. But, Wayne would continuously prove that he wasn't the person that Tom was looking for.

In his searches, Tom inadvertently became involved with a devil worshippers group. That group wanted to get rid of Wayne, because he was a threat to their existence. Wayne had the power to destroy all of the members and they had to get him first.

Naturally, Wayne Homza showed up and while he was freeing his friend Tom, the leader of the group, Donnavin flew in from California and a mental battle took place.

Tom is thinking about how he got his friend into this, how he really feels responsible. How he had seen things this night that could only come out of a nightmare. He feels that he has to make up to Wayne and his family somehow.

"Mr. Brinkle, here's your address book." The nurse says breaking Tom's thoughts.

"Will it be alright if I make the call to his mother? I can't give you that permission, but I'll see if I can find the doctor." The nurse leaves the room.

Ten minutes later the nurse returns with a doctor. The doctor walks up to Tom then shines a light into his eyes; he puts a finger up in front of his face.

"Tell me when my finger disappears." He then moves his finger back and forth and in and out with positive results.

"Well Mr. Brinkle, it's up to you, I don't think that there's

any permanent damage, nothing showed up on the X-rays. If you would like to leave, you're free to go. But I would like you to take a list of symptoms to look for, in case there is some damage that we couldn't find."

"That sounds like a good idea Doctor! I think that I will take you up on it."

"Okay, wait here until the nurse brings you the list back. And you will probably get some headaches out of this; simple aspirin should take care of it."

After Tom left his room, he went straight to a phone and started dialing.

"Hello, Mrs. Homza?"   "Yes, who's this?"

"This is Tom Brinkle. I unfortunately have some bad news for you-Your son Wayne was in an accident."

"Oh God no!   Is he alright?"

"He's in intensive care right now. The doctors said that he's going to be alright after a couple of days of rest."

"What hospital is he in?"

"Nanticoke."

"I'll be right down there." Then Mrs. Homza hung up the phone, shaken.

"What's the matter now?" Sue says as she enters the parlor, (Sue and her daughter have been staying with her mother since she and her husband broke up).

"It's Wayne; he was in some kind of an accident and is in the hospital."

"What? How did it happen, how is he?"

"I don't know, his friend, Tom just called and told me." Just then the phone rings again, Mrs. Homza rushes to pick it up.

" Hello?"

" Mrs. Homza?"

"Yes"

"This is Gail Cooper, your son's next door neighbor. Do you know where I could locate Wayne his wife just had a baby boy."

"What?"

Mrs. Homza has mixed feelings now.

"Wayne is in the Nanticoke Hospital, he was in some kind of accident."

"What should I tell Anita?"

"Don't tell her anything, I'm going to go down and see Wayne, and then I'll visit Anita, and tell her how he is. What hospital is she in?"

"Berwick."

"Thank you, bye"

" Bye"

Sue calls her sister Helene and asks her if her daughter could stay at her house overnight, Helene wanted to go along, but Sue told her that it would be a better idea, if she stayed at her house and called the other brothers and sisters. Sue said she would call her from Nanticoke, and let her know how their brother was.

At the hospital, Tom sees a familiar face exit the elevator.

"Tom, how's Wayne"

"You're going to have to ask the doctor over there. Doctor, this is Wayne's mother and sister."

"Hello Mrs. Homza" Said the Doctor

"Doctor, how is my son?"

"Well, I won't lie to you. When the paramedics found him, he wasn't breathing, but luckily there was a doctor at the scene and applied CPR right away, which kept the oxygen going through his system till they got him here. I finally revived him then he was breathing on his own. Right now, he's coming along just fine, but I don't know if there was any damage to his brain, as I don't know how long he went without oxygen,"

"What kind of accident was he in?"

"We're not sure; he was found lying outside a burning house, we think the furnace blew up,"

"Can we see him now?"

"Sure, but be brief."

Katrina Homza and Sue leave for Berwick Hospital after they had seen Wayne, Tom Brinkle leaves after his worried wife picks him up,

At the Berwick Hospital. Katrina and Sue see Gail at the window looking in on the new born babies. So, they stop. Gail points to the one with the name Homza tagged on the clear plastic crib,

"He's resting just like his father," Katrina thinks to herself, and a tear rolls down her cheek.

"How's Wayne?" Gail asks.

"The doctor said that he should be alright."

"I just didn't want to leave Anita here."

"That's alright, thank you for staying with her."

"You're welcome, I'll be leaving now."

"Okay, thanks again."

"Sure, Anita is asleep now; they gave her a sleeping pill." Katrina and Sue take a walk down to Anita's room, to look in on her and make sure she's alright. But as soon as she opens the door, Anita wakes up.

"Katrina? What's happened to Wayne? I know that something bad has happened to him and you know what it is."

"Wayne is in the Nanticoke Hospital, he was in some kind of accident, but the doctor said that he'll be alright." Anita starts to cry, Katrina walks over to Anita's bed.

"I know Anita; you know Wayne as well as I do that he'll come out of it, he always does."

"I know, but it is different this time. I sensed it as soon as he got that phone call, and had to leave. He sensed it too. I could see it in his eyes."

The next couple of days, Wayne's relatives and friends went to visit him. he would slide in and out of a deep sleep. Anita was released from the hospital after a two day stay. Katrina invited her to stay at her house, since it was in the city and someone could watch Wayne Jr. while Anita went to visit Wayne.

Wednesday, November 13, 1981. James and Helene was visiting Wayne, They were talking to him, because the doctor said that if they would talk to him he would recognize their voices, and probably come out of it. Helene was holding his hand talking about his new born son, when she noticed his facial muscles were twitching slightly.

"Look his face is twitching." James came walking over to his bed to see. Just then Wayne's eyes opened. They both jumped! He turned to face the two. Then, he started blinking as if he was trying to focus. Then he stopped blinking and started staring at them.

"Wayne, you're awake!" Helene said. Wayne's eyes started widening,

"Ahhhhhhhhhh! Wayne screams, then he pulls the blanket over his head and curls up into a fetal position noticeably shaking. James runs out of the door to get the doctor, while Helene trios to calm him down. The doctor enters the room with a nurse.

"What happened?"

"I don't know. I was talking to him then he got a frightening look on his face and tried to hide."

"Wayne Wayne. Its doctor Moss, we're not going to hurt you." The doctor said in a calm voice, as he sits on the bed and puts his hand on Wayne's shoulder.

"Leave me alone, go away." Wayne says in a childish voice. "What's the matter Wayne?"

"I'm afraid."

"Why are you afraid?"

"I want my mommy!"

"Nurse, go page Doctor Phillips, we need him stat."

"What's the matter with my brother, doctor?" James asks.

"I'm not sure. I sent for the resident psychiatrist." Fifteen minutes later, Doctor Phillips enters the room.

"Hello Doctor Moss, the nurse briefed me about the patient's state, is there anything else I should know?"

"No Doctor Phillips, the rest you'll be able to find out for yourself."

"Have you called his mother yet?"

"His sister Helene just did, she'll be here any minute."

"What are your names?" The doctor asks James and Helene.

6

"I'm Jim and this is Helene."

"Did you notice if he seemed to recognize you two?"

"No!"

"Would you leave us alone please?   As soon as your mother gets here, send her in."

Helene and James leave the room.

CHAPTER II

Be It enacted, that if any person shall use practice or exercise any invocation or conivration of any evil and wicked spirit, or take any dead man, woman, or child out of his or grave to be employed or used in any manner of witchcraft, enchantment, charm or sorcery, whereby any person shall be killed or destroyed, wasted or consumed, that every such offender, being of any of the said offended duly and lawfully convicted and attained, shall suffer pains of death.

STATUTE AGAINST WITCHCRAFT MASSACHUSETTS BAY COLONY

IF IT IS EVIL YOU SEEK,
THEN THAT IS WHAT SHOULD BE SOUGHT.
BUT, If IT IS EVIL THAT WHICH IS SOUGHT,
THEN IT WILL BE FOUND, AND IN THREEFOLD.

In the Heights section of Wilkes-Barre, there is a woman getting ready to dye the color of her hair. She has been known as Lavinia, but now she's going to change her name to Delfina. Her hair is long and jet black, she's going to color it blonde,

Lavinia came to Pennsylvania because of reports of a man with powers. Her master Donnavin wanted her to check out the reports and then get back with him. Well, she found out that the reports were correct. She, having powers herself, thought that she would be able to take care of him and that is what she told Donnavin, but he told her that he will take care of him personally. So, he flew in from California and she set the bait in order to get the man,

Lavinia never expected the man that she had looked up to and respected, would be defeated. She has never seen anyone who had as much power as her master. She knew that she had to continue with the group, and in doing so she has to change her looks slightly. The local people will follow her, or else she would have to hurt them, and they knew it.

In the Brookside section of Wilkes-Barre, a lonely Jeffrey Pelp, is .Just getting home from an irritating day at the office, Jeffrey was a bright student in school but an accident in grade school stopped him from doing any type of hard labor. So Jeff decided to use his mind to make a living. He went to college and majored in business administration.

For the last year it has been very depressing for Jeff. He would go out to the local bars, but not be able to pick up any women. But, he tries not to ponder on that thought too much, he pulls a TV dinner out of the freezer and puts it into the oven.

After Jeffrey finishes his dinner, he takes a shower and starts getting dressed to go out. Each time he goes through this ritual, he feels pessimistic about getting a girl.   Perhaps that's why he doesn't get one. He leaves his apartment about 8:00 p.m. and heads south on Washington Street he gets to Butler Street, he makes a left. He follows Butler Street a block then he pulls into the parking lot of a night club called "The Sabar."

Jeff walks into the plush bar, and sits at the bar.

"Hi Jeff trying again tonight, ha?" The bartender says.

"Oh hi Tony, yeah, maybe I'll get lucky tonight."

"What will you have tonight?"

"I'm going to have a change of pace with my drinks maybe it will bring me luck. Let me have a Margarita".

"Coming up."

Jeff sits at the bar just drinking his drink and watching the usual people walk in the door. Then the door opens and a woman comes into the bar out from under the outside light. Jeffrey watches her walk in and he feels strongly drawn to her, He scans her as a man scans a woman that he first sees. Her long blonde hair shimmering in the darkened bar, her dark eyes as she looks from side to side of the bar, her face soft and smooth like that of silk and her body which was molded by Venus herself. Jeffrey's heart starts pounding when she walks towards his direction, and when she sits down next to him, his palms were sweating profusely, and he began to shake, but quickly brought it under control.

"Buy a lady a drink?" The girl asked Jeff.

"Sure, what do you want" Jeff said, trying to hide his nervousness"

"Oh. I'll take a Bloody Mary."

"Tony, a Bloody Mary for the lady."

"Coming right up."

"My name is Jeff, what's yours?"

"Uh, Delfina."

"Delfina, pretty name." He looks into her eyes and seems to be hypnotized.

They engage in small talk till 12:15.

"It looks like it's getting late, Jeff. Why don't we go to your place?" Jeffrey was astonished at the request she made, even though it was exactly what he was thinking of.

"Sure, let's go."

All the way to Jeff's house, Delfina was staring at him, as if she was searching his mind for something.

They reached his apartment at 12:30 a. m.

"Well, this is it, it's not much but it's mine."

"It's a nice little place. What do your parents think about you living alone?"

"They preferred that I got out on my own. I don't have too much liquor here, but I could make you a Screwdriver."

"That'll be fine. Is that your class picture?" Delfina says as she gets up and walks over to a bookshelf and picks up an 8 x 10 picture.

"Yes, that's my second grade picture."

Delfina looks at it, then for no apparent reason she drops it.

"Oh, shit!"

"What's the matter?"

10

"I'm sorry; I thought that I recognized someone. Who is that?" She says as she points at a boy in the picture.

"Oh that's Wayne, I think his last name was Homza, or something like that. He came to school with old hand-me-downs, so the kids made fun of him all the time.

Now Delfina recognizes what it was she seen in Jeff, but didn't understand.

"Did you ever make fun of him?"

"Just once, but it was only because the kids were starting to make fun of me because I was his friend."

"In the bar you were telling me about an accident you had, was that around the time you were in second grade?"

"Yeah, I guess it was,"

Delfina sits next to him, and starts rubbing his groin area. Then she unzips his pants.

"Let's go into the bedroom Jeffrey." Delfina says in a very seductive voice. Jeff being very hot could only follow.

In the morning Delfina woke up, and started making them both breakfast.

"Hey lover what do you want for breakfast?" Jeff rolls over, then opens his eyes and notices that Delfina isn't in the bed.

"What?"

"I said, what do you want for breakfast?" Delfina says as she walks into the bedroom, giving Jeff a pinch on the buttocks.

"I'm too tired to eat right now."

"Come on get your lazy ass out of bed. It's not too often that you'll have someone cook you breakfast, so you might as well take advantage of it now."

"Okay, okay. I'll have a couple of eggs, sunny side up and bacon."

"Right, have your cute little ass ready in fifteen minutes," Jeff rolls over again thinking about going back to sleep, but he feels too intimidated to do it. So he sits up and then groans.

"Boy, that chick sure did wear me out last night. That was the first nymphomaniac I ever slept with." He thought to himself.

He gets up and puts on a robe, then walks into the kitchen and sits down, There was no way for him to know that she put some of her urine in a glass just after they got finished having sex. Some of her specimen was then mixed well with a spoon, then fried it with it the eggs.

"Is there any coffee made?"

"It's perking now."

"You want a glass of orange juice while I'm pouring some?"

"Yeah, go ahead and pour me a glass." "So, are you still a Catholic?" "Yes, I go to church every Sunday, why?"

"Oh, no real reason, it seems to me that you are wasting your time."

"What do you mean?"

"Well, instead of being in church you could be home making love," she says as she places his breakfast in front of him.

"Yes, but I don't want to go to hell."

"I'll tell you what, I'm having a party at my house tonight, why don't you come to it?"

"What time is it?"

"Come about ten o'clock."

"Okay. What did you do to these eggs, they taste very good. I've never tasted eggs like this before."

"I just added my special love!" Delfina said with a smirk.

After Jeffrey finishes his breakfast, he takes Delfina to her

house in the heights. Before they left, Delfina was trying to get Jeffrey into bed, but there was no way he could have sex that morning.

"Are you going to walk me to the door?" Delfina says as he pulls up in front of her house.

"Sure."

When they get to the door Delfina grabs him, and gives him a long wet kiss. Also grabbed and squeezed his buttocks. Since it was Saturday, Jeffrey went back home and went back to sleep. He couldn't help thinking about this strange woman that suddenly entered his life. It was as if she was sent to him.

As soon as Delfina got into the door, a guy and a girl walked up to her.

"Lavinia, where were you, we were waiting all night for you to show up." said the guy. Delfina walks up to the guy and grabs him by the shirt. Don't ever question my actions again, and from now on my name will be Delfina, got it!"

"I got it, Delfina."

"Now let's get down to business. Is the room set up?"

"Yes, we set it up last night." "Good, let's take a look at it."

They walk into the dining room, where there isn't any furniture. Delfina looks on the floor where she sees a large pentagram.

"Let's take up position. She says to the other two. They move to the middle of the circle, then they kneel holding hands, they bow their heads and concentrate.

"Master" Delfina says as she releases all her power, trying to conjure her master.

"Damn that goody two shoes, I swear on Donovan's body that I'll get that son-of-a-bitch, if it takes me the rest of my life." Delfina screamed in anger.

"Don't let it get to you, we'll get him, but it'll take time."

"But I don't even sense that Donovan still exists!"

"I was there when he destroyed our first leader, before you came and I definitely want to get revenge. But you know as well as I do that we have to wait."

"I know, what did your friend at the Nanticoke Hospital have to say?

"As far as she could find out, he is due to be release any day now."

"What about his friend, the news man?"

"He was released the same day that he was admitted."

"Could your friend get in to see him?"

"No, she's only a candy striper. She already tried." "Well, at least we still have our ace in the hole." Ten o'clock, Jeffrey arrives at Delrina's house. After he parked his car, he went on the porch, he was ready to knock on the door, but he noticed that the lights weren't on. He checked the number again, but it was the right one. So, he knocked on the door. It took about five minutes, and he was ready to leave, but as soon as he started to walk away, someone came to the door.

"Yes, can I help you? Oh, you must be Jeff. Hi! I'm Linda, come in."

"Where's Delfina?" Jeff looks at the girl that came to the door, she looked like she was only seventeen years old. She had short brown hair, and green eyes. She had some kind of black silky robe on. Jeff could tell that she didn't have a bra on under the robe.

"Delrina's in the other room. Can I take your coat?"

"Okay, what's that smell?"

"Incense, you like it?"

"Yes."

"Follow me."

Jeff follows the girl through the darkened room. Just before they get to the dining room, Linda presses Jeff against the wall with her body grinding her crotch against his and starts kissing him. Jeff pushes her away,

"What are you doing, suppose Delfina sees you?" All Linda did was laugh.

The both of them went into the dining room. Jeffrey had an amazed look on his face. He looked around the room and saw allot more people in those black robes. In the middle of the room was a table with a naked girl on it. He felt apprehensive, and wanted to leave, but something was holding him there. He looked and saw Delfina in the middle of the room.

"Jeff, come join me." His legs started walking, but he didn't want to. He reached her.

"Jeffrey, I want you to join our group."

"What is it all about?"

"We could give you power beyond your wildest belief."

"Why me?"

"Because I like you."

"You are devil worshippers aren't you?"

"No, we believe in the Masters. The ones that created the earth, and had it robbed from them."

"Who are they?"

"You'll find out in due time."

Jeff looks into Delrina's eyes, and feels controlled by her. He now feels much more at ease.

"What do I have to do?"

"See that girl on the table?"

Jeff looks at the table, and sees a young girl chained to a table with her legs spread apart.

"yes"

"You have to fuck her, she's a virgin."

"I changed my mind Delfina, I don't want to go through this." Jeff looks up at her and says, "But she doesn't want to do it." Delfina starts kissing Jeff, while unbuttoning his shirt. The other members of the group started chatting quietly. Jeff just feels spellbound, and was getting very horny. Delfina made him feel the girl's tits while she was kissing him.

When he was stripped naked, Delfina started kissing the girl licking her nipples, then sucking her pussy, she then kisses Jeff so that he can taste her juices until he gets very turned on. He starts moving over to her and starts having sex with her. The other members of the group start chatting in rhythm with him. The girl tries to pull away but chains hold her down. With tears in her eyes, she tries to plead with him. But right now he has no conscience.

After it was over, Delfina got a small tin cup and caught the blood

14

that was dripping out of the girl. Jeff now was feeling bad about the whole thing. Delfina put the cup up to his lips without letting him know that it was the blood, and made him drink it. She then drank some, and passed it around to everyone else. Then they all took their robes off and started an orgy,

The next morning he woke up and noticed that it was after one o'clock. Then he thought about last night. It all seemed a dream until he looked at his stomach and saw some dried up blood. He went into the bathroom and was ready to turn on the shower when the phone rang.

"Hello."

"Jeff, why weren't you at church today?"

"Hi mom, I just woke up, late maybe I'll catch the later mass."

"I thought that you were sick or something."

"No, I'm alright. I've got to go and take a shower now, bye." and he hung up. He knew that he wouldn't catch the later mass. He just couldn't, not after last night.

After he gets out of the shower the phone rings.

"Hello."

"Hi there sexy."

Jeff has a weird feeling come over him.

"Hi Delfina."

"How are you feeling this afternoon?" "Strange."

"That's normal, we're having another party tonight and I would like you to be there."

"I don't know. I have to go to work tomorrow."

"Don't worry about work, you'll get there. Just be at my house about the same time,"

Delfina hangs up, and then turns to one of her followers.

"Get the book out and ready for tonight."

"Are you sure you have to go to such an extreme, as using that book?"

"Yes. I have to use that book; it is the only way left." Jeffrey arrives at the house at ten o'clock. The house is dark like the night before. He knocks on the door, this time it's answered almost immediately.

"Hi lover, come in."

"Hi Linda, I'm not late am I?"

"Sort of, there's a lot of stuff we have to do tonight. Here, put this robe on,"

"Over my clothes?"

"No, you have to take your clothes off."

"All of them?"

"Yes, it's to show that we don't have anything to hide. Put it on quickly, we're in a hurry."

She stares at his every move while he was removing his clothes.

"Just leave your clothes there, and let's go," When they arrive to the dining room, Jeffrey notices that it was different. In the middle of the floor were two circles of flour, and in the middle of that was a tin bowl with weird engravings on it. Inside the bowl was bread, pine resin, and some weird looking grass. Next to the bowl was a copper looking dagger, Delfina walked up to him, and took his hand,

"I have a job for you lover boy." She took him to the center of the circle.   "Sit down next to that bowl, and pick up that dagger."

Delfina then lit the contents of the bowl. After that she

picked up an old thick book and handed it to him. He put it on his lap, and looked at its name. "NECRONOMICON"

"Turn the page that I have marked and get ready to repeat the words in it."

The other members back far away from the circle, and one goes to the light switch, standing ready for a cue from Delfina.

"Now Jeff, you're going to have to read that by the fire light, because we're going to turn the room lights off,"

She then nodded, and the lights went off,

"Start reading now, Jeff."

"IA MASS SSARATU!   IA MASS SSARATU!   IA MASS SSARATU ZI KIA KNPA!   BARRGOLOMOLONETH KIA! SHTAH!"

All of a sudden Jeff saw a weird looking dog appear outside the circle. It started to growl then walked back and forth, as if it was standing guard outside the circle. Delfina walks over to Jeff, and turns the pages to find another invocation.

"Now read this one."

"BAADANGARRU!   NINNGHIZHIDDA!   THEE   I INVOKE, SERPENT OF THE

DEEP!   THEE I INVOKE, NINNGHIZHIDDA, HORNED SERPENT OF THE DEEP!   NINNGHIZHIDDA! OPEN! OPEN THE GATE THAT I MAY ENTER!

NINNGHIZHIDDA, SPIRIT OF THE DEEP, WATCHER OF THE GATE REMEMBER!   IN THE NAME OF OUR FATHER, ENKI, BEFORE THE FLIGHT, LORD AND MASTER OF THE MAGICIANS, OPEN THE GATE THAT I

MAY ENTER! MAY THE DEAD RISE AND SMELL THE INCENSE!"

A male figure starts to form inside the circle. Everyone is quiet, and watching what is happening.

"The one you wish to appear cannot be found. I came in his place to answer any questions you may have."

"I am Delfina, slave to the master. I want to know how to take revenge on the master's death."

"Is this the body that you have chosen?" The spirit says as he points to Jeff.

"Yes, this is the body."

"You made a very good choice. Continue to initiate him into your group; the rest will be controlled by us. I will let you know when we come in contact with your master, and then you'd have to return him here. Is that all?"

After the figure had permission to leave, he disappeared.

Then Jeffery broke his trance and became afraid, and got up to try and leave the circle. But, just as soon as he moved towards the boundary the trans- parent dog hunched down and gave out an eerie growl. Delfina grabbed Jeff and pulled him back to the center of the circle,

"You must never leave the circle until you send the watcher away."

"Okay, what do I do to send him away?"

"You have to repeat these words,"

She hands him the book, turned to a different page, Jeff sits down next to what fire was left in the bowl and started reading. But first, Delfina put his hand on the sword,

"BARRA MASS SSARATU! BARRA!"

Then the dog disappeared, and the fire went out,

"Turn the lights on." Delfina said.

CHAPTER III

WHEN YOU ARE A CHILD,
YOU TRY TO THINK LIKE AN ADULT.
WHEN YOU ARE AN ADULT,
YOU TRY TO THINK LIKE A CHILD.
TO YOUR PRESENT AGE, HOLD ON BEFORE IT IS
FOREVER GONE.
FOR IF THEY LEAVE AND YOU TRY TO RETREAVE,
YOU MAY REMAIN THAT AGE FOREVER.

Wednesday, November 18, 1981. Katrina Homza is walking down the hallway of Nanticoke Hospital to visit her son. When she approaches his room, she notices her son and daughter standing outside his room.

"Mom, I'm glad you showed up!" Helene says. "Why, what's the matter?"

"Wayne woke up and acted as though he didn't know us", Jim said.

"The doctor wants to see you in there right away."

Helene interdicted. Katrina with a puzzled and worried look on her face rushed into her son's room,

"Mommy!" Wayne sat up just as soon as he saw his mother enter the room.

"Wayne?"

Katrina rushed to his bedside, hugging him.

"Mrs. Homza, I'm Dr. Phillips, the staff psychiatrist."

"Why does my son need a psychiatrist?"

"He has somehow regressed to an earlier age,"

"What? How?"

"He must have suffered a great trauma before he went unconscious. We will know more when we know what exactly happened at that house."

"Wayne, how old are you?"

"I'm ten years old mommy, you know that"

"Yes. I know, I just wanted you to tell the doctor."

"I don't like it here mommy, I want to go home."

"You will as soon as you're better."

"Mrs. Homza, may I speak to you over here?"

"Sure, I'll be right back Wayne."

Katrina walks over to the far side of the room where the doctor is.

"He didn't recognize his brother or sister. You're going to have to introduce them to him."

"What about his wife?"

"You're going to have to say that she is his sister also"

"I still don't understand how something like this could1ve happened."

"The mind is extremely complex; we still don't understand what makes it work."

"What do we do about Wayne?"

"The Shickshinny State Hospital is closed down; you're going to have to send him to the Hazleton State Hospital. Perhaps they will be able to help him."

"I can't afford to send him to any hospital."

"But, they have been treating patients with similar problems since they opened."

"How many did they cure?"

"Naturally they made limited progress, everyone can't be cured,"

"You didn't answer my question."

"There was a small percentage cured. But, they've got better techniques now."

"Don't you think he'd be better off if he went with me, and both his wife and I took care of him."

"Yes, I think it would be better for him, but most people could only handle it a couple of days, then they put the patient in a state hospital."

"Well, I've taken care of my children, and then my grandchildren. I'm sure I could take care of my own son until he's feeling better. Now I'm going to bring his brother and sister in, then explain it to his wife."

"Okay, but we're going to be keeping him here for a couple of days for observation. I'll come in periodically for sessions."

The hardest person Katrina had to break the news to was Anita. But after that had been done, Anita was glad that her husband was still alive. She knows that there's always a hope that he would return to normal.

Sunday, November 22. 1981. Wayne Homza is being released from the hospital today. Anita Homza is there to pick him up along with Katrina and Wayne Jr.

"Wayne, this is your sister Anita, and her son Wayne."

"He has the same name as me."

Anita put her arm around Wayne, trying to hold back her emotions. When they got to the house, Katrina showed Wayne where he'd be sleeping. Anita and a couple of members of his family had already brought his clothes from his trailer. Just as soon as Wayne settled in he went to the attic, where he found some cars that belonged to his nephews, and started playing with them.

An hour after they arrived home there was a knock on the door. Katrina went to answer it.

"Yes, oh hi Tom. Come in."

"Thank you Mrs. Homza. I heard that Wayne was released from the hospital today, so I thought that I'd come by to see him. Is there any change?"

"No, there isn't any change. Tom, you've got to tell me what happened in that house."

"I'm sorry Mrs. Homza. I can't. You know Wayne so you could just about guess what had happened."

"The doctor said that he might be able to help him if he knew what happened."

"I don't think so, you know Wayne, he has to work it out himself. Besides, even if I did tell the doctor what happened, he wouldn't believe me, Can I see Wayne?"

"Yes. I think he's in the attic." "Thank you."

Tom Brinkle went up to the attic.

"Hi Wayne."

"Hi, you're the man that came to see me in the hospital, aren't you?"

"Yes, my name is Tom."

"Hi Tommy, do you want to play cars with me?"

"Okay, I'll play with this one."

"No, I'm playing with that one, you play with this one!"

Wayne said as he grabbed a fire engine off Tom.

"Okay, I'll play with this one then."

"No, I changed my mind."

"Wayne do you remember me at all?" Wayne looked up at him and stared.

"Yeah, you're the man that visited me in the hospital. I already told you that!"

"I know that, but do you remember me from before the hospital?"

"No! I thought you were going to play cars with me."

"I am. I am!"

Tom Brinkle stayed in the attic and tried mentioning things to trigger Wayne's memory but all it did was irritate him, so Tom gave up after a half hour.

After Tom Brinkle left, Wayne got tired of being up there all alone, so he decided to go down stairs. When he reached the upstairs hallway, he went past a bedroom, and he heard crying coming from the room. So he stood by the door then opened it. He looked in to see Anita lying face down on her bed crying. She didn't notice that anyone had walked into the room. Wayne walked up to her and put his hand on her back.

"What's the matter Anita?"

She rolled around on the bed, because she recognized the voice.

"Wayne, I thought you were playing with your cars."

"I was but I got tired of it. Why you crying?"

"I think I lost someone that I love very much."

"Where did he go?"

"I don't know, he's just gone."

"That wasn't nice of him to go away like that and make you cry!"

"I know, but I can't do anything about it."

"Well, if I find him, I'll beat him up for you."

"Thank you, Wayne." Anita said as she reaches up to kiss him on the cheek.

At nine o'clock Wayne went to bed. He dressed into the pajamas that his mother bought him while he was in the hospital. It was an exhausting day for him. He was running around with what seemed to be endless energy. So, he went to sleep right away.

Eleven o'clock Anita was in her room sleeping, Sue was in her room sleeping, and Katrina was downstairs watching T.V. When they all heard a very loud shrill, come from Wayne's room. Katrina bolted up the stairs, Anita and Sue shaken out of their wits opened their doors. All three of them rushed into Wayne's room. Katrina turned the light switch on, but the light wouldn't go on. She kept on switching it on and off, till it finally went on. When the light went on, Wayne stopped screaming. He was just sitting up in bed staring with a glaze in his eyes. Katrina went over to him and started shaking him by the shoulders.

"Wayne are you alright! Wayne!" Then Wayne snapped out of it.

"Mommy! What's the matter? What are you doing in here?"

"You must have been having a nightmare so back to sleep Wayne." Wayne looked at the worried look on their faces, and heard a baby crying.

"Your baby is crying, Anita."

They left the room, and Wayne slept peacefully the rest of the night. The next day Katrina called Dr. Phillips at the hospital. She waited until the page brought him to the phone.

"This is Dr. Phillips, can I help you?"

"Doctor Phillips, this is Mrs. Homza."

"Yes, Mrs. Homza is there anything wrong?"

"Wayne woke up last night and started screaming very loud; when we got to him he was sitting up in bed in some kind of daze."

"Did he recognize you?"

"Not right off. I had to shake him to wake him up."

"I don't know what to tell you Mrs. Homza. It seems as though he was just having a nightmare But, it could be more than that, I could come over on my spare time and try regressive hypnosis again if you'd like. But, as of yet, I had no success with him."

"Maybe this time it would work. I also wanted to mention that when Wayne was around ten or twelve years old, he never acted this way. He was ready and willing to take on responsibility. He wanted to grow up fast. But, now he just wants to stay a child."

"Perhaps he's just reliving his childhood doing something he missed the first around."

"When will you be able to come over?"

"I should be there somewhere around five o'clock."

"How about if you stay for dinner?"   "Yes, I guess I could."

"Fine, I'll see you here then."

5:15 Doctor Phillips shows up at the Homza's residence. Katrina answers the door.

"Hi Dr. Phillips, I'm glad to see that you could make it."

"I got held up in traffic, but as you could see I made it."

"Wayne is out in the backyard somewhere playing, would you like to talk to him now?"

"No, its best that I wait till after dinner, he'll be more relaxed then."

After dinner Dr. Phillips asked Wayne to show him his room. Wayne looked at his mother and she gave him a nod. So, the two of them went up to Wayne's room,

"Wayne, where is it that you want to be more than any place else?"

"Oh, I don't know, maybe in the skies like Star Trek"

"Okay Wayne, have a seat over there."

Wayne went over to a cushioned chair and sat down. Doctor Phillips pulled up a desk chair in front of him.

"Now Wayne, we're going to play a game. Close your eyes and imagine that you're on the bridge of the USS Enterprise. Think Wayne, look out the windows of your mind and see the stars passing by." Doctor Phillips said in a monotone voice.

"Relax Wayne, look at the stars zooming by. You are now lighter than air floating around on a spaceship. Now you're back to your eighth birthday party. Do you see your cake; you're ready to blow out the candles?"

"Yes, I see it."

"Look around you, see your brothers and sisters. Now you're

older you're fourteen, and its Christmas morning. Do you remember?"

"It's a little fuzzy. Everything is blurry."

"Everything is clearing up now. It's not blurry anymore. Tell me what you got for Christmas."

"Yes, I could see it now!" Wayne said with   excitement in his voice.

"It's a pool table. I bribed my brother Jimmy to tell me. I was out shoe shinning and they put it together for me in my room.

They had the lights out so I couldn't see it, but I saw it."

"Very good, now we're going to move into the future once again. You're now twenty-four. You're in a house in Nanticoke; it is Friday, November 13. 1981. Tell me what you see?"

"I can't see anything, its black!   The room is starting to spin! I'm getting dizzy!"

Wayne starts shifting around in his chair.

"Wayne! Wayne! on the count of three you will snap out of it. One, two, three. Wayne!"

The doctor yells real loud. Then Wayne finally comes out of it. The doctor checked to make sure Wayne was alright, and then went down stairs.

"What happened Doctor?"

Katrina runs up to him to ask, as soon as she saw him. "Well, I had a little more progress. But, he still has some kind of block separating him from what happened on the thirteenth. I believe with regular hypnotic treatments that he will eventually break through that mental block.

Katrina made some arrangements for the doctor to return whenever he could. The doctor said that he couldn't charge her anything. After the doctor left Wayne went into Anita's room.

"Hi Anita."

"Hi Wayne, what's on your mind?"

Anita was hoping for the reply of hair. That's what Wayne used to say to her, when he was in a joking mood.

"Oh nothing much. I was just thinking, I remember most of my brothers and sisters now, but I don't remember you. Why is that?"

"Oh, I don't know, maybe because I wasn't here much then."

"Oh!"

2:00 a.m. everyone in the house was sound asleep, except one person. Lying awake in her bed, Anita couldn't help but think about her husband in the room down the hall. She finally gets out of bed, and walks down the hall to his bedroom. She turns the doorknob so as not to wake him up. Then she pushes the door open very slowly. Then she was frozen by fear in her tracks. She wanted to turn and run but was paralyzed. She was staring at the apparition of a young beautiful woman with blonde hair. In an instant she knew who it was. She saw enough pictures of her. "Phyllis" She said to herself. Just then Phyllis turned her head from Wayne and looked at Anita. But her look was so gentle, Anita didn't feel scared anymore. Phyllis gave Anita a look of acceptance, then disappeared.

CHAPTER IV

THERE ARE DIFFERENT MEETINGS THAT WE HAVE TO CONTEND WITH.

THERE ARE MEETINGS OF THE MINDS, THE MEETINGS OF THE BODY, THE MEETINGS OF DEFEAT, THE MEETINGS OF VICTORY, THE MEETINGS OF AN ENEMY, THE MEETINGS OF A FRIEND, AND THE MEETINGS OF DEATH.

Wednesday November 25, 1981. Jeffrey Pulp hasn't been feeling himself lately. He broke off connection with his family, walked around with glazed eyes and felt dizzy, stumbling around without ever noticing it, and almost fell a couple times.

After Jeff came home from work, he went straight to bed. As he lies there in his bed, he starts thinking thoughts which aren't his own. His slight trance gets broken by the ring of the telephone. He hesitates to answer it. There is a small force within him which is rebelling against answering it. But he can't fight it and knows that he must answer it.

"Hello."

"Jeffrey darling, how are you doing?"

"Oh hi Delfina, I'm doing okay."

He automatically falls under the spell of her voice.

"I would like you to join me and my friends tonight." Jeff's stomach turns,

I

"What time do you want me there?"

"Come the usual time, around ten,"

"Okay. I'll be there."

Jeff hangs up the phone, and dozes off. He has never had so many nightmares as he had for the last week. Even as he doses off he tosses and turns, due to bad and scary dreams.

Jeffrey awoke to a cold sweat. He got out of bed, and took a cold shower. After that he started heading towards the Heights. Traffic was light tonight; it only took him a half an hour to get to Delfina1s front door. When he knocks on the door, a different girl answers. She motions for him to follow her. They go into that same room, Jeff sees everyone on the floor looking as though they were praying. Jeff gives the girl his coat, then takes his pants off, and lets the black gown which was tucked in his pants, hang down. He walked into the room, and walked up to the altar, where Delfina was deep in concentration. As Jeff got near her, her concentration broke, and she focused on him. She then got up and went to get the Necronomicon, Jeff sat down to face the congregation. Everyone else remained concentrating.

Delfina brings the book over to Jeff, who already is in a trance. She opens it to the right, and starts handing it to him, but he puts his hand against it.

"That won't be necessary Lavinia."

Delfina stops amazed at what she just heard.

"Yes Lavinia, it is I, your master."

"Master!" Delfina replies as she bows down to him.

"You can rise now. What has happened while I was away?"

"Our group is now growing in strength. After that night, the weak ones left, but the strong ones remained and helped me to rebuild this area of our group." The other members were coming out of their trance-like state. Fear entered their bodies and took control, they couldn't move, they remained sitting.

"What did you do to your hair?" Donnavin asks.

"I died it blonde and changed my name to Delfina, so that I would not be readily recognized."

"And where is Mr. Homza now?" Donnavin asks with malice in his eyes.

"He survived the battle, but was hospitalized. It is said that when he woke up, he had the mentality of a ten year old.

"How good is your information?"

"It's very good."

"Is he still in the hospital?"

"No, he was released last Sunday."

"I need to find out what state of mind he is in."

"That should not be too much of a problem. The body that you are in went to school with him."

"That's good; I cannot under estimate him again. If he has in fact regressed to that state of mind due to the battle. I will be able to destroy his body before he regains control of it. But if he's trying to draw us into a trap, I will be able to react accordingly."

"How long will you be able to hold on to this body?"

"I'm not sure. I am drawing strength from you and the others right now. Until I regain my original strength, I will have to be going in and out of it. While I'm away, I will see what his eyes see, and hear what he hears.

"Will Homza know that you are connected with this body?"

"No. when he goes to visit Homza, I will be far away, Homza will never know that I survived, and I want to keep it that way,"

"When do you want Jeffrey to visit Wayne?" "Tomorrow, the sooner the better,"

The meeting broke up and all the members walked up to Donnavin one by one, and kissed his feet to welcome their master back. What they had seen, had strengthened their belief in what they were doing,

Thursday, November 26, 1981, Wayne wakes up to the smell of

pie baking in the oven. He gets dressed and goes down stairs. He sees Katrina Sue, and Anita getting things ready for the Thanksgiving turkey that they're going to have this afternoon,

"Wayne, why don't you go into the parlor and watch the parade on TV" Katrina said.

"But, I want to watch you bake the pies and stuff."

"Now come on Wayne, you're just going to get in the way." Katrina puts her arm on Wayne's shoulder and leads him into the parlor, then turns the TV on.

"Now sit there and watch the parade."

Katrina starts to walk back to the kitchen, when she hears a knock on the door.

"You want me to get it, Mom?"

"No, I'll get it Wayne."

She walks over to the door, and then opens it.

"Yes, may I help you?"

"Mrs. Homza, I'm Jeffrey Pulp, I went to school with Wayne. I was wondering if you could tell me where he lives. I'd like to look him up for old times' sake."

"I'm sorry Jeff; Wayne hasn't been feeling well lately."

"Who is it Mom." Wayne interrupted.

"Hi Wayne, remember me."

"No" Wayne said as he shook Jeff's extended hand.

"We went to school together, Jeffrey Pulp"

"I'm sorry, Jeff, I told you he wasn't feeling too well lately."

"I'm sorry. I'll come back some other time when he's feeling better."

After Jeff left, Wayne went back into the parlor and watched T.V. Jeffrey Pulp walked back to his home. Delfina and some of the members were waiting for him.

"What were you able to find out?" Delfina asks as soon as Jeff walks into his apartment. Then his appearance seemed to change; his posture straightened up, his face tightened, and seemed to gain ten years in a minute.

"He has truly regressed. I couldn't sense any power what-so-ever. Now we're going to have to act fast, and destroy him before he regains his wits!"

"How did he get that way?" Delfina asks.

"He must have gone into shock, due to the traumatic experience of our fight. He must have been so drained that he withdrew inside himself. And that's more of a reason to act fast."

"How do you want us to dispose of him master?" One of the

members asked.

"Basically, we're going to have to play it by ear. I cannot participate in it. He must not know that I survived the battle. Stake out his house and wait till he comes out to play then one of you will have to approach him, and convince him that you are his friend, once that is accomplished, get him into your car. Then I want you to take him to baby road there you will meet with more of your brethren. Delfina, you know how to set it up."

"Yes master, but what about his kid? Wouldn't he pose a threat to you also?"

"I was just coming to that. After we finish with him, we're going to have some more of the brethren drive by his house and throw in gas bombs."

"Why don't we just throw gas bombs in their house while they're all asleep tonight?" The same guy asks.

"Because if he sees that his family is in danger, he might return. And I don't want to provoke his return that is why I want him separated."

"Jeff broke up the meeting and went into his bedroom to lie down. But not before he dispatched the men to stake out Wayne, and Delfina to set everything else up.

4:30 p.m. The two men were sitting across the street from Wayne's mother's house. Snow flurries were starting to fall. The two men were just about to give up when they saw Wayne walk out the door. They watched as he walked down the street all bundled up for the cold weather. The men waited until he got far enough away from the house, then the one on the passenger side of the car got to catch up to him. The other man pulled off and drove up the road to turn around.

Wayne just got out of the house to enjoy the falling snow. He was tired of his brothers and sisters showing him pictures that he didn't recognize. And talking about places and times that he couldn't remember. So he just let the brisk November air hit his face while he walks down the street.

"Wayne, Wayne wait up."

Wayne turns around and sees a man that he doesn't remember seeing before. But, since he knew his name, Wayne thought that he'd wait for the man to find out what he had to say.

"I'm glad I caught you in time. I was just at your house, and your mother told me that you had just left."

The man says as he approaches Wayne. Hoping that Wayne didn't see him get out of the car.

"How do you know my name?"

"Why I'm your Uncle Tom, don't you remember me?" He says watching the expression on Wayne's face.

"No. I don't remember you."

"Well. I'm your father's brother, and he gave me a message to give you."

He says as he gets ready to pour it on thicker.

"What is the message?"

"Your father would like to see you.   He sent me to pick you up."

"Why didn't he pick me up himself?"

"He's not feeling well. He wanted to see you in case something happened to him."

Just then he gave a signal for his partner to pull up.

"Are you ready?"

"First I have to tell my mom where I'm going."

"I already did, she said that it was alright."

"Okay, let's go."

Wayne got into the back seat of the car, and they drove away. After a while Wayne started noticing that they weren't driving towards his father's place.

"Hey Uncle Tom, we're not going to my dad's house."

"No, I forgot to tell you. Your dad is staying with me for now."

"Oh, I see."

5:00: Now it is dark out, and the roads were wet from the snow flurries. The car Wayne is in just pulled up on baby road. They continued to drive on it until they came to a dirt road, then they make a right turn on it. They follow that road down until they come to a clearing. The driver turns his lights off then on again, then off again, then drives down with only his parking lights on. The vehicle then comes to a stop.

"Where are we?" Wayne asks.

"We have just come upon your doom. Now come on out you little bastard."

"No, I don't want to."

But before Wayne could lock the door, the big guy in the front grabs the door and flings it open. He grabs a hold of Wayne, and pulls him out. Wayne lands on the ground, then gets up and starts to run. A set of headlights come on in front of him, he then sees a man with a pipe in his hands start walking towards him. So Wayne starts to run in another direction, and another set of headlights come on.

Wayne could hear a chain rattling. He turns to run another direction and yet another set of lights come on. Then all of a sudden, there is a circle of cars around him with their headlights on, and people moving towards him with weapons.

Wayne looks around, and sees that he is in a wooded area and that he can't escape. The people were moving very slowly toward him, almost as though they were enjoying his fear. The first man was five feet away from Wayne, with a tire iron cocked, and ready to strike him. Then all of the headlights went out all at one time. With this black, moonless night, everyone's vision was impaired; Wayne leaped into the air, and gave the guy closest to him an ace kick to the chest. The guy goes down in a groan, Wayne starts to make his way to one of the cars, when he bumps into another guy, Wayne grabs him by the right arm, turns around, (which turns him around) then flips him on his back. Then he notices another guy coming he lets out a front snap kick to the groan then one to the face as the guy bends over. He starts hearing a scuffle from behind him, but continues to make it to one of the cars, until he finally makes it to one. He gets inside, turns the light switch off, and then turns the ignition switch. The engine roars to life. He then turns the light switch back on, and sees the guys fighting with themselves. When they notice what was happening, they run to their cars and tried to start them. The batteries seemed to be dead; Wayne put his car in reverse and stepped on the gas. Pebbles were knocked up from under the tires and spread into the faces of the guys chasing after him. They throw their chains and pipes out at him, but to no avail,

8:30 pm Vincent Hand and Marilyn Zigger are leaving a house in the heights of Wilkes-Barre, They get in a car, 1972 Mustang II, and start driving off making sure the box in the back is secure. They get onto East Market Street and travel west until they come to the square. They follow the circle half way around, then take a right on North Main street, The streets are half deserted, because people are home belching up their turkey, Marilyn could drive that Mustang almost as good as Vincent, But of course Vincent taught her.

"Hey Vinny, do you think that this will be enough stuff to kill them all?" Marilyn says as she takes her mind off of the driving to ask the question,

"By the time we get there, they should be in the living room watching T.V. So, that's where I'll throw the gas bomb. They won't have enough time to run out, their first thought will be for the

32

kids sleeping upstairs. If any of them reach the stairs, by the time they get up there the whole house will be on fire, so they're as good as dead,"

"Can we ditch the car afterward and come back; I want to see the charred bodies,"

"I have to anyway, Delfina said to make sure that none of them survived, most of all the infant!"

As they pass North street, Vincent started thinking of the days when he was a little league pitcher. He feels as though he could have made it to the major leagues, if only he had half a chance. But his pitching arm will be used tonight. To pitch a couple of bottles filled with gas, and a rag sticking out of the neck of it,

"Do you think he's dead yet?" Marilyn asks, breaking Vincent's train of thought, Vincent looks at his watch; ten till nine,

"I don't know, They wanted to have fun with him before they finished him off. He's at least messed up by now,"

"I wish I could have been there to watch,"

"Well, you get to see his family burn. Just like in the Salem witch burnings."

Marilyn continues her concentration on driving. She notices that she just passed Butler Street and knows that she was getting close to the house.

"Now remember, slow down when you get a couple of houses away, and then I'll get out, light a couple of bottles at a time, then throw them through the window. After that we'll get the hell out of here."

Vincent said with an authoritative voice. Marilyn could feel excitement creep into her bones. She would remember the times she saw her cat's kittens and stomp on them, feel their bones crunch under her shoes. At first she started feeling sorry for them, but then she started liking it. This will be the first time she caused a human to die, and she is looking forward to it.

Wayne pulls off the dirt road, onto baby road. He then realizes where he's at and knows what's going to happen if he doesn't get home before hand. He's driving a 1968 Station Wagon. The sides are full of rust because of the cruel Pennsylvania weather, and all the salt that is placed on the roads after it snows. The engine is burning oil and needs a tune up badly, but Wayne manages to get it going fast enough to hopefully get him to his mother's house on time.

Anita is impatiently sitting in the living room waiting for her husband to get back home. She was thinking that in his state of mind he has never stayed out past nine o'clock. And it was five till and she hasn't seen him yet.

Wayne finally reaches Main Street, it seems as though it took him forever to get there. He made a left on Main and traveled south. Two miles up the road, a Ford Mustang II is traveling north getting closer to their objective. Wayne floors the gas pedal and puts his high beams on. He sees another car in the opposite side of the road coming towards him. The car flashes its high beams off and on to try and get him to dim his. He ignores it, and continues. His car and the car ahead were the only two on the road. Wayne knows who was in the car ahead of him and why.

When he gets to be a hundred meters away from the other car, he moves over into its lane, then opens the door and rolls out. Ten seconds later there is a big explosion, and bits and pieces of a Mustang and a Station Wagon were flying everywhere. Wayne manages to crawl off and hide until he's able to walk.

Anita sitting in the Living room with Katrina and Sue watching T.V. suddenly hears an explosion. They get out of their seats and go out on the porch to find out what it was. Anita hoping that Wayne wasn't involved was the first to go out the door.

"Go call the police!" Katrina shouted to Sue.

"The line is busy, Mom."

"Someone else must have called them already." Then Katrina looks at Anita.

"Don't worry, it just looks like someone lost control, and ran into another car,"

After an hour the excitement was over with the fire department came and put the fire out with foam, then the police department had the cars towed away after the remains were removed from the Mustang.

Anita tried but she couldn't get to sleep. Thinking about Wayne worried her. She called the police, but they said that they couldn't do anything until he was missing for twenty-four hours, and that he wasn't near any of the cars that were wrecked. They searched all over the general vicinity, and found no one. 3:00 a.m. she finally fell asleep.

Wayne woke up with pain and sore muscles. He looked around and noticed that the streets were empty. He could smell gasoline in the air. The ground was freezing up, except where he was sitting. It was very cold, but his butt was keeping it from icing up. He got to his feet and started walking to his mother's house. He looked at his

34

watch 3:15.

He went around to the back door, because he didn't want to wake anyone up. He opened it slowly, then entered and closed it behind him. He made his way up the stairs (his thigh muscles hurting with every step) and went straight to Anita's room. As soon as Wayne entered Anita's room, he went over to the crib to see Wayne Jr.

"I was gone for a while son but I'm back now."

"What? Who's there?" Wayne heard a sleepy voice say. "Wayne!"

Anita gets up and runs into Wayne's arms.

"Where were you, I was worried."

Wayne didn't say a word; he just pulls her away, and then kisses her; like he never kissed her before.

"You're normal! You're normal!"

Anita says after the long kiss that she has been waiting so long for. Then the glare of the night light shows the dried up blood on Wayne's face.

"What happened? Are you alright?"

"I'm alright, I just need some rest. I'm going to lie down before I fall down."

Anita helped Wayne get undressed. He fell asleep as soon as his head hit the pillow. He was sound asleep but his dreams were filled with nightmares. They went back to the day of his battle. Then once again he was in Phyllis's room, and the orderly told him that she was dead. Tears streamed down his face, in his silent slumber.

Back in Jeffrey Pulp's apartment, Donnavin is enjoying the body of Jeffrey Pulp, and the human desires. He and Delfina just got finished having sex. Then he bolts upright.

"He's back!"

"What, whose back?"

"That bastard returned."

"Wayne returned to his body?" Delfina asks in a puzzled voice.

"Yes, and he's taking care of the followers that were supposed to kill him. Our attack actually woke him up!"

"Can't you interfere?"

"No, if he found out that I was back, he'd destroy me for sure." "What can we do?"

"Nothing, maybe Vincent and Marilyn will reach his mother's house before he can stop them.

Donnavin waits for a time that seemed to be forever. Watching through his third eye. He knows that Wayne can't see him watching him, and that Wayne has to be pretty weak himself, but not half as weak as he is now. Then, he sees Wayne racing towards his mother's house. He thought about making the station wagon stall out but he knew that Wayne would feel it, and so he was helpless when he saw the crash.

"They're dead." Donnavin said with a sigh.

"Who, his family?"

"No, Vincent and Marilyn."

"Oh no, how do we stop him now?"

"You just continue to recruit as many as possible. We will have strength in numbers. I will let this worthless body get close to him, then I will enter it when he is least expecting it. One way or another he will have to be destroyed, so I could go ahead with my plans to take over the government,"

"We don't want to make much bigger of an impact on this town. It's a pretty small town they were pretty upset when a new religious organization entered it."

"Yes, but your group members helped to spark the turbulence, which started the whole thing. What you do is start with the city officials, and their families. Then if there is an uprising of any kind the officials will use their double talk to talk the citizens out of it. It is always good to have the people under control."

The next day Wayne slept till well past noon, Wayne Jr.

wouldn't allow Anita that pleasure, though. As soon as she heard him crying, she got out of bed and picked him up, so that her husband wouldn't be awaken, Anita put the crib in Sue's room, after getting her permission. She wanted Wayne to sleep as long as he wanted to, undisturbed. Even though, deep down inside she couldn't wait to hold him and talk to him again,

When Anita heard Wayne move around on the bed, she knew that he was almost ready to get up. She went to the bedroom and opened the door slowly. His head was in her view, and she could see one eye open and looking at her,

"Are you going to get up, or sleep some more?" Wayne rolled over to his side with a grunt, Anita could see that he was in pain,

"I think that I'll get up. Would you please put some hot water in the tub for me?"

"Okay,"

No one was in the house, except for the three Homza's, After Anita told Sue and Katrina the news, they were very happy, and decided to leave Wayne and Anita alone, to get reacquainted. And that they did.

Wayne painfully sat up. Every part of his body was in pain, either from a bruise or a cut. He felt like the day after he first started lifting weights and pushed himself too far. He started to stand up when Anita came into the room.

"Need help?"

"No, I think I could do it. Where is everybody?"

"They went shopping."

"Oh, is the tub filled?

"Yes"

"Good," Wayne said then went into the bathroom, closed the door, urinated then took his clothes off after he flushed the toilet and put the lid down. He then opened the door, and stepped into the steaming hot water. He slowly lay down in the tub; he could see Anita getting clean clothes for him in his bedroom. She then brought them into the bathroom and put them on the closed toilet seat. She looks down at his body, and sees the hideous bruises all over his body. She gets a disgusted look on her face. Wayne notices the look, and figures that he has to say something.

"They're only bruises,"

"I know, but there's more to it than just bruises."

"Anita." Wayne says as he grabs her hand tenderly. "I had to do what I had to do."

"Were you in that accident last night?"

"Yes sort of"

"But, there were two kids killed in that accident!" Wayne looked down at the water.

"Yes, I know. They were coming here to throw fire bombs at the house."

"Fire bombs! Why?"

"Because on the thirteenth of this month, I had a fight with a very powerful person, I won, but as a result I was in the shape that I was."

Wayne hesitates to look at his wife. She has a bewildered look on her face. She knows enough about her husband to know that he isn't making it up,

"There was this occult group of Satanists that called him in, They were renting that house in Nanticoke, They found out that I was staying here, and knew what condition I was in. They have people working everywhere, even in the hospital. So, they decided to take me into the woods and beat my skull in. Then, they were going to take care of my offspring, so that they would have no problem with the Homza's anymore,"

"You got to go to the police and tell them everything!"

"Then for sure I'll end up in a whacko house!"

"Show them what you could do, make something explode. That'll convince them,"

Wayne looks down into the water again. Then looks up at her,

"I can't,"

"What do you mean,"

"I've strained myself in the fight. Let's not talk about that now. Wash my back for me, okay,"

Wayne and Anita made love that afternoon in the true sense of the word, Wayne Jr. was just laying in his crib in another bedroom, playing, But when his parents started having intercourse, he got sort of a smirk on his face, as though he was pleased,

Saturday, November 28, 1981, Wayne woke up, and got out of bed.

He's still very sore. Anita was already out of bed, giving Wayne Jr. a bath. Wayne went down stairs to get his breakfast,

"Morning honey" Anita says as she picks up Wayne Jr. out of the baby tub.

"Morning."

"Would you like me to fix you some breakfast?"

"No, go ahead and finish with Wayne." Katrina came into the kitchen now.

"How are you feeling today, Wayne?"

"Not so great Mom. I feel like I've been run over with a steam roller."

"I have some aspirins if you want some."

"No thanks mom."

"You want me to make something for you for your breakfast?"

"Thanks mom, if it wouldn't be too much trouble."

"Eggs over medium, right?"

"Yeah, and some fried mashed potatoes if you have it."

"We have some from dinner yesterday."

"Anita, what did you tell them at work?" Wayne said changing his attention to Anita.

"Well, they knew that you were in the hospital, I told them that it would be a while before you recover. Your doctor, Dr. Phillips backed up my statement with a report. But he didn't say anything specific."

"What did they have to say?"

"They couldn't promise anything, but they would try to hold your job open as long as possible."

"Well, I'll find out on Monday. Oh mom, we'll be moving out today."

"Are you sure?"

"Yes, we discussed it yesterday. We're going to go back to the trailer, I have enough money in the bank to last for a while, if I don't get my job back,"

"If you think you know what you're doing,"

All afternoon Wayne was busy loading his car up with their stuff. His brother, Jim worked a half day, so he helped Wayne with allot of his stuff.

After the accident of the thirteenth, Tom Brinkle picked up Wayne's car from Nanticoke and brought it to Wayne's mother's house. All Wayne had to do was go into the backyard to get it; Wayne was ready to start it up, when there was a knock on Katrina's front door. So, Katrina went to see who it was,

"Oh hi Jeffrey, Wayne's out back just getting ready to leave,"

"Thank you, Mrs. Homza." Jeff said, and then went out to the backyard;

He sees Wayne, his wife, and his baby in his Buick. Wayne Jr. becomes very wrestles and starts to cry.

"Wayne!" Jeffrey shouted.

Wayne looked over and saw Jeff with a hand in the air. Jeffrey walked over to the driver's side of the car.

"Hi Wayne, how are you feeling today?" Wayne looked at him, then recognized him.

"Oh hi Jeff, I'm feeling alright. How about yourself?"

"I'm doing okay. Are you moving?"

"Yes, I was only staying here until I felt better."

"We ought to get together some day and have a beer, so that we could talk about old times,"

"Yes, we'll do that," Wayne said but never really meant it.

"Well, let me give you my address and phone number." Jeff scribbled on

a piece of paper. Then handed it to Wayne.

"Could I have yours?"

"I guess," Wayne took the note book that Jeff offered him, and put his address and phone number on it.

"I will be giving you a call soon," Jeff said, then left.

"I don't like him, Anita said, I wouldn't trust him,"

"Right now I don't trust anyone. But, I guess I'll listen to your woman's intuition, that's all I have to go on right now,"

It took Wayne and Anita the rest of the day to clean the trailer and thaw out the water pipes. When they finished Wayne decided to call a friend to let him know that he was alright.

"Hello."

"Tom."

"Yes, who is this?" "Wayne."

"Wayne! are you alright?"

"I am now, I'm back at my trailer,"

"That's great! How about you and Anita coming over for dinner tomorrow?"

"That sounds like an enterprising idea, wait till I clear it with the Misses,"

Tom hears muffled talking.

"Tom."

"Yes."

"Is it alright if we bring Wayne Jr.?"

"Sure, my wife would like to see him."

"You got yourself a date."

The next day, Wayne visited their friends in the trailer park. All of them were glad to see him; and he them. He needed the exercise of going from trailer to trailer. Even though it hurt him to do all that walking, he still did it. It helped him to think about what he was going to do in the future. The day turned cold and cloudy when the afternoon came around.

At six o'clock Wayne, Anita and Wayne Jr. pile in his Buick and start heading towards Tom Brinkle's house. They arrive at six-thirty-five. Wayne parks his car as close to the house as he could get, and grabs Wayne's 'fold up crib, and carries it to the door. Anita carries Wayne Jr.

"Come in Wayne, Anita." Tom says as he opens the door.

"Oh what a handsome baby!" Tom's wife says as she walks over to greet the supper guests. Is meatloaf alright?"

"Sure, I like meatloaf." Wayne says, and then notices his wife giving her approval to Mrs. Brinkle,

"You could set the crib up over here, Wayne." Tom says pointing to a spot near the kitchen.

"Okay" Then Wayne sets the crib up.

Tom's children get along pretty well with Wayne Jr. While the grownups were enjoying a before dinner wine, the kids were playing with Wayne Jr., making him laugh. 7:15 they all sit down for dinner.

Meatloaf, mashed potatoes, and green beans.

"So Tom, how is the job coming along?" Wayne asks while he butters his bread.

"Oh, it's coming along fine. There's always news to be found. How about you, are you going to be able to get your job back?"

"I don't know yet, I'm going to call them on Monday."

No more was spoken during dinner about Wayne getting a job. After dinner Tom gave his wife a cue to take Anita upstairs and talk to her about womanly things. He wanted to talk to Wayne alone.

"So Wayne, what are you going to do if you don't get your job back?"

"I don't know, I have some money in the bank that'll last me for a while. After that I should already have a job.

"As I said, in my job there is a lot of news happening. So I get first hand information on what is going on."

"What are you leading up to, Tom?"

"There have been a lot of kids disappearing lately. There is one lady in Kingston willing to pay five hundred dollars for anyone that could locate her missing daughter."

"That money would come in handy, but I doubt I would be able to find her daughter, more or less find my way home."

"Wayne, I saw what you could do, if anyone will be able to find her daughter you will!"

"Do you know what being burned out feels like?"

"You mean a person burned out on drugs?   No not really."

"Well a person burned out on drugs becomes useless, that's the way I feel right now.

"What do you mean?"

"I burned myself out that Friday.   I even had to leave my body because of the damage I would have done to my brain if I stayed."

"Will you be able to get your power back?"

"I don't know. That's not my worry right now. That group tried to kill me and my family the other day."

"Go to the police, I'm sure that they'll help you."

"I doubt that very much, don't forget that I haven't been exactly sane lately, plus I don't know where their new house is. They probably have a couple of them by now."

"Maybe the girl's disappearance bas something to do with them."

"Yes, I thought of that when you mentioned it. How old was the girl?"

"She was fifteen."

"That would be right, she's probably a virgin."

"I don't know if you could find too many virgins, even at the age of fifteen."

"Apparently they did. I'll tell you what, get as much information that you can on all of the people that have disappeared within the last couple of months, and I'll get back to you on Monday."

"Okay Wayne. I'll do that."

Monday Wayne woke up at eight o'clock just to call his former employer. And his results were less than he expected. He knew that they couldn't hold his job open permanently, but he thought that they'd hold it a couple of weeks. His body was still hurting, so he went to bed for a couple of hours.

At eleven o'clock, Wayne was awaken by the phone ringing.

"Wayne, it's for you." Anita said as she came into the bedroom.

"Okay babe, thanks. Hello."

"Wayne, this is Tom, so how did you do with your old boss?"

"Not so well Tom Of a matter of fact, I struck out."

"I'm sorry to hear that, did you consider my proposition yet?"

"Yes, I could use the extra money, so I guess I'll give it my best shot."

"That's great, are you going to tell Anita?"

"I guess I'll have to, I can't lie to her."

"I don't think that she's going to like it."

"I don't think she will either. All that she's been through, I don't blame her,"

"Well here's the scoop. There are three people reported missing, A girl fifteen (that's the one I told you about) another girl fourteen, and a boy sixteen, I asked the T.V. station to let me follow up this story, They finally gave me the assignment,"

"Okay, I'll meet you at the Big Boy restaurant in Kingston in about an hour, order a pot of coffee and two cups. We're going to go over everything that you know then,"

Wayne hung up the phone after telling Tom Brinkle that he should be there in an hour or so. Then, he went into the kitchen to get something to eat,

"Who was that on the phone?" Anita said as Wayne walked by her,

"That was Tom, He was telling me of a way to make some money,"

"What happened to your old job?"

"I don't have it anymore, they couldn't hold it,"

"That's great, what type of work are you going to be doing with

Tom?" "Locating missing people,"

"How are you going to be able to do that, especially since the cops can't?"

"The cops don't know the right questions to ask, I do. Besides I already have a general idea where they are."

"Does it have anything to do with that occult group?"

"Yes it does."

"Wayne I don't know if I could take anymore of this worrying about you. And suppose something happens to you?"

"Anita if that group is still out there, and causing the disappearance of these kids, then they have to be stopped before they get too big, Don't forget that they still have to get rid of me, and my family, I have to stop them before they get that chance,"

"Why don't we just move away, we could stay in New Jersey,"

"Running away won't solve the problem, just prolong it,"

"You want to do this, don't you?"

"In a way, yes. But you have to understand, I love you and my son, I don't want anything to happen to you two. They know me and what I'm capable of doing. They can't have me or you two alive." Wayne takes her into his arms.

"I also have to think about the kids that are missing, and the ones that will be missing in the future."

"Well Wayne, do what you think is best. You will anyway. All I could say is be careful, and that I love you,"

After a long embrace, Wayne left for Kingston; He didn't get a chance to eat at home, so he decided to get something while at the restaurant. As soon as Wayne entered the restaurant, he saw Tom Brinkle sitting in the far corner, away from everyone else. It reminded Wayne of whenever he went out with a girl. Because that's the kind of place he'd sit so they could talk. When the hostess walked up to Wayne, he just told her that he was to join a friend, and then pointed to where Tom was sitting. She acknowledged and followed him over with a menu.

"Your waitress will be over in a minute,"

"Thank you," The hostess walked away, so Wayne turns his attention to Tom,

"I didn't get a chance to eat, so I'm going to grab a bite here,"

"Okay, you want coffee?"

"Sure, Boy winter is coming,"

"Yes, I know, I had trouble starting my car!"

"Are you ready to order?" The waitress says as she walks up to their table,

"Yes, I'm going to have a Big Boy sandwich, French fries, and Cole slaw,"

"Will that be all?"

"You want anything Tom?"

"No thanks, I already had something while I was waiting for you,"

"Okay, your order will be coming right up,"

"Thank you, now Tom we've got to get down to business,"

"Did you tell Anita?"

"Yes, I had to."

"What did she say?"

"Oh, she didn't like the idea, but I explained to her what would happen if the group expanded,"

"Well what do we do first?"

"First we go talk to the parents, then we have to do a lot of detective

work,"

"I'm used to that, I had a talk with my boss and told him that I have someone working along with me, and that this someone has a nose for news, I asked if he'd put you on the payroll to work along with me,"

"What did he say?"

"He said that he was going to see what kind of progress we'll make on this assignment, and then decide."

"Well, thanks a lot for asking; I guess that was a fair answer,"

The waitress brought Wayne's order over, and Wayne ate without really saying much. He was thinking of what exactly he was going to say to the missing girl's parents.

Tom called the missing girl's house while Wayne was eating dinner, to see if they would be able to talk to one or both of them. Her mother was home and said that it would be alright if they came over this afternoon. Wayne finished his dinner, left a tip, then the two of them left for the missing girl's house. With the afternoon traffic it took them twenty-five minutes to reach her house. She was living in the rich section of Kingston. They arrived at her house and walked up to the door. Tom knocked on it. It took two minutes, and then a middle aged woman answered the door.

"Mrs. Robinson?"

"Yes, you must be Mr. Brinkle."

"Yes, this is Wayne Homza, he'll be helping me."

44

"Mr. Homza." Mrs. Robinson says as she nods to him.

"Mr. Brinkle you look different from on T.V."

"That's the make-up."

"Well come in."

They walked in and sat down on the couch.

"Would you like a cup of coffee or something?"

"No thank you Mrs. Robinson, we just came from a restaurant and had more than enough coffee there. But, we do need to ask you some questions."

Wayne said pulling a small pad out of his coat pocket.

"Was your daughter acting different or strangely before she left?"

"She was quiet, and to herself. But there wasn't anything really noticeable."

"Do you know her boyfriend, and where he lives?"

"Yes, he's a nice young man. The police already talked to though."

"Yes, I realize that, but there are some questions that I would like to ask him,"

"His name is John Fisher, he lives at 1098 Pringle."

"I have one more question Mrs. Robinson; do you think she ran away from home?"

"No I don't think so, we may have our problems, most families do, but it wasn't bad enough for her to run away,"

"Okay, well we have got to get going, thanks a lot for your patience and information. Do you think that I'd be able to get a picture of Doreen?"

"I might have another picture of her here; I had to give the police a picture of her too. Wait a minute; I'll see if I could find one,"

Mrs. Robinson went up stairs to her daughter's room, and then a couple of minutes later came back down.

"Here's a school picture of her, I hope it will help you,"

"Thank you Mrs. Robinson, I'm going to try my earnest to find Doreen, And when I do, you could be assured of hearing from me as soon as I would be able to get to a phone."

"I sure hope that you will be able to find her Mr. Homza, I want this nightmare to be over with as soon as possible,"

Wayne and Tom left and were on their way to see Doreen's boyfriend. For the first time since Doreen was missing her mother was able to find hope in her daughter being found. Then the horror came to her thinking what shape she could be in.

Wayne and Tom waited until school was out, then went over to John Fisher's house. When they knocked on the door, his father

answered it,
"Yes,"
"Mr. Fisher, I'm Tom Brinkle from the channel 16, and I would like to talk to your son; John if possible."
"Is whatever he has to say going to be on T.V. or anything like that?"
"No, I'm just an investigator reporter. I'm investigating the disappearance of Doreen Robinson."
"Wait here, I'll see if he'll want to talk to you." Mr. Fisher left the two standing on the porch. Then returned five minutes later with a tall slender boy with black wavy hair.
"John, this is Mr. Brinkle and I didn't catch your name."
"Wayne Homza."
"And Mr. Homza, they're from channel 16. They just want to ask you some questions."
"Okay, what do you need to know?"
"You want to walk with us; I could talk better when I'm walking." Wayne speaks up.
"I guess that will be alright."
All three of them start walking down Pringle Street.
"So John, what do you think happened to Doreen?"
"I think that someone kidnapped her. Her parents aren't poor, you know."
"Yes, I know. Did you notice if she was going through any change?"
"Come to think of it, yeah. She seemed to be distant, far away. But, I thought it was me. We were fighting a lot lately."
"What were you fighting about?" John looked down and didn't want to answer that question.
"John, I know what it's like in school. You have to lie in order to be accepted, even if it hurts people. Did you actually have sex with Doreen?"
"No I didn't. You're right I did lie. But everyone else was telling about their experiences, I couldn't say that she wouldn't let me touch her tits more or less screw her."
"Well don't worry about that now. Just tell me about Doreen, what was she like?"
"She liked excitement. Even though she was quiet and shy, she would always go looking for a new thrill. She wore conservative clothes. She's sort of old fashioned. She is very stubborn. There's not

46

much more I could say to you."

"Did you ever see her talking to different people? People that you've never seen before, or don't know"

"Yes, once. When I asked her about him, she said that he was just a friend."

"Do you have anything of hers that she gave you?" "She made herself a beaded necklace, she gave it to me one day after we got into an argument. It's this one that I have around my neck."

"Can I see it for a minute, please?"

"I guess, if you give it right back, I don't make it a habit to take it off." John took the beaded necklace off and gave it to Wayne. Wayne grabbed it and walked away, then motioned for Tom to continue to talk to John.

Wayne walked off and sat down. He could hear Tom's and John's voices behind him. He held onto the necklace and started concentrating. It felt good to him, as though he didn't do it in a very long time. He closed his eyes, then started to see images. They were blurry at first then they started to come in clearer. He saw a girl, a young girl in a wooded area.

There were people standing around her. He could see that she was crying. He got the impression that she was in danger. He seen her drinking something from a tin cup. There was a cabin in the background. Then the word truck came in his mind. Then he lost the image.

Tom and John started walking towards Wayne. John was wondering what Wayne was doing with his necklace. He wanted it back. Wayne gave him his necklace back then they all started walking back to John's house.

"I hope I helped you guys."

"I'm sure you did John." Tom said looking at Wayne to see if there was any reaction. After Wayne and Tom finished, they went into Tom's car and Tom drove towards Wayne's car.

"Did you get anything?" Tom was the first to speak.

"Yes. they're keeping her in a wooded area."

"There's woods all over here!"

"I know, but that's all I could see, except that there was a cabin in the background. Then I got a feeling that she was in danger, after that a truck, and then they bury her in the woods. It would be a long time before anyone would be able to find her."

"What do you want to do now?"

"I have to get home, I feel a doozey of a headache coming on."

"You said that she's in danger, don't you think we should talk to some more people and try to find her."

"It wouldn't be any good, once my headache comes, all I could do is sleep."

"Alright, if you say so, I'll come by your trailer in the morning."

Wayne got into his car and went home. By the time he got there, his headache was beginning to blur his vision. He got out of the car and went into the trailer. Anita wasn't there, but her car was, he figured that she'd be at one of the neighbor's so he went to his bedroom and lay down.

Ten minutes later Anita walked into the trailer with Wayne Jr. She put him into his crib, and then went into the bedroom. She saw her husband lying on the bed, asleep. She was wondering whether she should make supper or not. She decided to wake him up to find out.

"Wayne, Wayne."

Wayne opens his eyes. Anita could see that they were glossy and his pupils were dilated. She knew that he had a bad headache. The kind he used to get by healing people.

"Did you take any aspirin Wayne?"

"No, I just need some sleep."

And he closed his eyes, then went back to sleep.

Thursday, December 3rd, 1981. Wayne is sound asleep in his bed. It is now 3:05 a.m. and Wayne begins to dream.

The last couple of days, Wayne and Tom were talking to Doreen's friends at school. But Wayne couldn't come up with anything. He was feeling depressed and felt that he was trying too hard.

In his dreams he's driving, but he's going in slow motion. He passes a read sign, and looks at it, but a big refrigerator truck was blocking his view. He wanted to see where he was, and where he was going. He pulled over to ask someone where he was, but no one would tell him. All he could remember seeing on that sign was ville. They carried him to a cliff then threw him off. He could see the ground coming closer and closer, and then he woke up in a cold sweat. He looked around and noticed that it was only a dream so he rolled over and went back to sleep.

7:00 a.m. Wayne's alarm clock went off. He woke up then turned it off. Anita was already out of bed feeding Wayne Jr. Wayne walked into the kitchen.

"You had a rough night last night." Anita says turning her

attention to her husband.

"Yes, I'm worried about that girl."

"You tossed and turned all night, how could you do that girl any good if you don't get any sleep?"

"I'm going to have to go by determination, I guess. I didn't even notice that I was tossing and turning that much."

"Is Tom stopping by this morning?"

"Yes he is."

"I have a pot of coffee on; do you want me to make you something to eat?"

"Yeah, go ahead, I'll finish feeding Wayne."

"Okay, after he eats give him his formula. It's already made up." At 8:00 a.m. Tom showed up at Wayne's. Anita answered the door.

"Hi Tom, how's Jean?"

"Hi Anita, Jean's fine. How about you?"

"Oh, I'm doing fine. Wayne's in the bathroom, he'll be out in a minute. Have a seat in the kitchen. I'll get you a cup of coffee."

"Thank you."

After sitting and chatting for awhile, Wayne and Tom left in Wayne's car. They got on route eleven then headed towards Kingston. Once they arrived in Kingston. Wayne just drove down Wyoming Avenue, and then came up on Route 309, he slowed down, then turned left.

"Why are we going down here, there isn't anyone that she knows down here,"

"I know but I'm just driving around."

Wayne continues to drive down 309 then for some unknown reason the highway looked familiar in a different way he saw the sign, the dream comes back to him.

"Tom, look at that sign,"

"That sign that we just passed, what about it?"

"What did it say?" "Trucksville"

"Trucksville, that's it. That's where she's being held!"

"Well step on it, let's find the place!"

Wayne comes to the first and only stop light in Trucksville then takes a left. He drives down the road, trying to miss the pot holes. Then he slows down, he sees a dirt road to the right, thinks about it, and then turns on it. He looks at the sky and could see that it was very cloudy. The weatherman threatens snow. He comes to another dirt road and makes another right. He follows it a mile than makes a left. He goes down a mile and a half then stops, because of a large tree in the middle of it.

"Is this the wrong way?"

"No, it's not. We have to walk from here,"

"But there aren't any other cars. There's no sign that anyone has been here,

"Trust me and let's go, we don't have a moment to waste," The two men got out of the car, bundled up their coats, and started running. Wayne's legs ached because he hasn't really ran in a long time, but it felt good. As they were running they could hear chanting in the distance, it was very low but as they got closer, it started getting louder.

Wayne is in the lead, he continues to run until he comes outside of an occult circle. Wayne stops, then Tom stop besides him and look in horror.

Wayne and Tom are standing there with steam coming off their mouths. Then they see a naked girl on what looked like a stone table. Someone with a hood on (one like the KKK wears, but black) is standing beside the table with a dagger in his hands ready to thrust it between the girl's breasts.

"It's got to be twenty degrees out here, and that girl's naked!"

"Not by choice, I'm going to run up and get that guy away from her. I want you to put your jacket on her, then untie her, I will try to keep everyone away from you two. Here's the keys to my car, get her to the car, and if I can't follow take off. Take her to the nearest hospital."

"But   —"

Before Tom could say anything, Wayne had given him his keys, took his coat off, and started running. Wayne was a couple of feet away from the guy with the dagger, when he yelled right before he was ready to plunge the dagger into her chest. Then Wayne leaped, waited until he was just in front of him, then let out a thrust kick to the throat. The guy's Adam's apple was crushed immediately, and was dead before he hit the ground. Wayne's coat fell lightly on the girl and was in place before Wayne landed.

Tom came running out of the woods as soon as he saw Wayne leap. He made it to the table and placed his coat to the bottom half of the group. Then he reached into his pocket for his trusty pocket knife. And thought about the sales pitch. It's made for many uses. He wondered if they hadn't considered it being used for this. And it might save a life someday. He cut one of her arms and one leg loose. Then he felt an arm around his throat, he couldn't get loose from it.

50

He tried frantically to pull it away but couldn't. Things started getting black.

After Wayne landed, he looked around and saw the guards that were posted in the woods come running out after him. The first guy that reached him tried to rush him, so Wayne stepped aside, stuck his foot out then used the guy's forward momentum against him, and made his head rush into the stone table. Wayne heard a loud crack. The next guy stopped short of Wayne, so Wayne used a double front snap kick, one to the groan, then the next to the face. Then Wayne turned around, and saw that Tom had someone on his back, Wayne ran around to the back of the guy then kicked him a paralyzing kick in the small of his back. The guy collapsed right then and there,

Wayne held onto Tom, until he caught his breath, and then looked around, everyone else was staying back from Wayne, a teenager came running through the crowd, and stopped in front of him, he pulled out a switch blade. Wayne could tell that he was a street fighter, and knew how to use it.

After Tom was able to see clearly, he picked up the girl after he cut the other two ropes. He looked over at Wayne, seen the guy with the knife, then Wayne looked at him.

"Get the girl out of here!   Now!"

After Wayne yelled at Tom, the guy with the knife lunged forward, trying to catch Wayne off guard, Wayne noticed it out of the corner of his eye, and tried to grab the guy by his wrist. And at the same time move out of the way. But he wasn't quick enough, and was punctured slightly, in his side. Wayne immediately backed from the knife, the guy could see anger in Wayne's eyes when he touched his side and got blood on his hand. Wayne took a step forward, and did a round house kick, knocked the knife out of the guy's hand, then came around with a back wheel kick, and hit the guy in the temple with his heel. The guy hit the ground hard. Wayne leaped towards him, then threw a straight punch between his eyes.

Wayne got up and looked at the crowd. Some of the people in it recognized his anger. They seen it before, when he destroyed their leader, it seemed like ages ago. The ones that knew him started running towards their cars. Then the rest lost their prowess and joined in.

Wayne walked back to his car, and a sting was constant in his side. He finally made it to his car, he noticed that it was running and that Tom was inside, the girl was in the front seat sitting in a daze. He got inside the car. Tom had managed to button the coat up behind the girl. Wayne looked her over carefully, he saw that her lips were purple and she was shivering.

"Will she be alright, Wayne?"

"I don't know, she's drugged, but that stopped her from going' into shock."

Wayne put his finger tips on her temple; then turned her head towards him. Tom looked at them and was thinking about the show Star Trek. Spock's Mind Probe. Wayne's eyes turned motionless, dull. He was concentrating, her breathing became deeper and slower. Her pupils were going from pinpointed to getting larger. Tom put the car in reverse and started backing out.

When they finally reached the hospital, Tom pulled up in the emergency zone, and then rang the bell at the door, while Wayne started pulling Doreen out of the car. Tom came back over and helped Wayne with Doreen. They reached the door and an attendant opened it. She went back to grab a wheel chair, then they went into the emergency room. Tom went in to explain what happened, while Wayne called Doreen's mother.

Fifteen minutes later, the police arrived. Tom called the T.V. station and they sent a crew down to the hospital. Doreen's mother arrived with mixed emotions.

The doctor walked out of the emergency room. Mrs. Robinson walked up to him immediately.

"Doctor, how's my daughter?"

The cops, Wayne and Tom walked up to the doctor to listen to his answer.

"We had to pump her stomach out. She was filled with Seconal." Mrs. Robinson looked at him in a weird way.

"Reds, Amphetamine, Downers."

Mrs. Robinson nodded to show that she understood.

"How is she going to be?"

"It looks like she's going to make it. Her body was rejecting the drug in an amazing rate. We're giving her warm sponge baths."

"When will I be able to see her?"

"After her bath, we have to make sure frost bite hasn't set in anywhere."

Wayne and Tom finished making out the report, then showed the police exactly where it was that they found the girl. The police couldn't find it themselves. When they arrived at the place, they were surprised to find that there weren't any bodies at all there. By now the snow had fallen and there was two inches on the ground.

The detectives showed up, and started looking around. Then they came across a couple of holes, but they were empty. After that they came back to the table, and found splattered blood at the base of it. After a couple of hours of going over the story with the cops, telling them that they couldn't reveal their sources, the cops finally left them go.

After all that, no one noticed the blood stain on Wayne's shirt. Except for his wife, Wayne got home, took a hot bath, and then got a massage from his wife, after she bandaged him up. Wayne's headache came after the massage, he just went to bed.

CHAPTER V

WHEN YOU HIDE BEHIND YOUR MASK,
YOU COULD ONLY DO THAT WHICH IS TASKED.
REMOVE IT FOR ANOTHER ONE,
FOR YOU WILL HAVE ANOTHER TASK TO COME.
OUR TRUE SELVES ARE HIDDEN WITHIN,
AFTER TOO MUCH USE THE MASK GETS WORN THIN.
WHEN IT GETS THIN,
AND YOU KNOW YOU CAN'T WIN.
REMOVE IT FOR ANOTHER.
ALL PEOPLE, LIKE CLOWNS, WEAR MASKS.
SOME TO HIDE THEIR FEARS, SOME TO HIDE THEIR ANXIETIES, SOME TO MISLEAD OTHER PEOPLE. THE MOST DANGEROUS ONES ARE THE ONES THAT HIDE TO MISLEAD OTHER PEOPLE.

Saturday, December 19, 1981. Wayne's wound healed up pretty well. His wife was insisting that he get a couple of stitches in it, but Wayne refused to go to the hospital.

Wayne started exercising again. He broke out some weights, and bought some more. He started running again, and working on strengthening his stomach.

Nine o'clock in the morning, Wayne got out of bed to answer the phone before it wakes up Wayne Jr.

"Hello."

"Wayne, Tom, I've got some good news for you!" "What's that?"

"You've got a job as my assistant."

"That's great! I'm getting tired of sitting around the trailer all day."

"I took a look at the official report, how about if I come over and discuss it with you?"

"Sure, come on over."

Wayne's attempt to catch the phone before it woke up Wayne Jr. failed. He had to pick up his son while on the phone. After he hung up, he changed Wayne Jr. and sat him in his high chair with a few things to play with; He heated up his son's baby food. He thought that he'd let Anita sleep in this morning. After he fed Wayne Jr., he put him in his crib to play with the different things that were hanging just above him.

As Wayne was doing the dishes, he saw Tom's car pull up in his driveway. He dried his hands off, and opened the door just as Tom was beginning to scale the steps.

"Come in Tom" Wayne said as he opens the door.

"Boy, its sure cold out there, you'd think that winter was here already instead of a couple of days away."

"Yeah, I know. Have a seat." "Don't mind if I do. Where's Anita?"

"Oh she's still sleeping. She had a tough time sleeping for some reason last night. So, what was the official report?"

"You know them holes that they found?"

"Yeah."

"Well, they checked them out and found that each hole was a point of a pentagram. They suspect that they were going to cut up that girl and put a part of her in each hole,"

"That's barbarous!"

"I know that's why we have to try to stop these fanatics." Wayne got up to get Tom a cup of coffee, when the phone interrupted him,

"Hello."

"Wayne, this is Jeff. Are you going to be busy today?"

"I'm sorry, I can't remember who you are."

"Jeffrey Pulp you and I went to school together."

Thursday, December 3, 1981. It didn't take long for word to get back to Delfina.

"What do you mean someone disrupted your ceremony?"

"Two guys broke in and tore up the place, they even killed a couple of our guys,"

"Who were these guys?"

"One was that Wayne fellow, the one that blew up our last leader."

"Call the house in Dallas, PA. Immediately, and have them help clean up the bodies and whatever else you could, before the police get there."

Delfina hung up the phone, and then waited impatiently for Jeffrey Pulp to get home. As soon as he walked into the room, she jumped up and walked over to him.

"Donnavin!"

"I know about the Trucksville incident."

"What are we going to do about it?"

"Do you remember Steve Brodie from California?"

"You mean that guy from the mafia? The one that wanted to use the power to get to the top?"

"That's the one; I'm going to cash in a few favors."

"You're going to try a hit man, but Wayne will sense the danger!"

"Yes, I know, but he will back off for a while. Don't forget he has a family to care for,"

"What about Brodie? Won't he be killed?"

"More than likely, but he was trying to take over leader in our house there while you're gone. He even tried to kill someone. Besides, Wayne is crowding us too much. We need time to get stronger,"

"So, you want me to call him?"

"No, I already did. He's going to be busy for awhile for the mafia. As soon as he's finished, he'll be here. In the meantime, Jeffrey Pulp will have to get Wayne's confidence."

Thursday December 17, 1981. Jeffrey Pulp had to continue his job as to not create more suspicions. His soul is being more and more tormented by the spirit of Donnavin. He has no real control over his body anymore. It's either dominated by Donnavin or

Delfina. As soon as he walks through the door of his apartment, Donnavin enters his body.

"You get anything from Brodie yet?" Donnavin said to Delfina looking down at her on the couch.

"Yes, he called this morning from Ohio. He's driving here, and said that he'd be here around five o'clock."

"You gave him directions to the apartment."

"Yes."

5:30 P.M. There came a knock on the door. Delfina got up to answer it.

"Lavinia! How are you doing you old slut?"

She looks up to see a tall husky guy about 6'2", black hair, and his face looked like his teenage pimples never went away, He reaches down and lifts her up, his large biceps bulging.

"I'm going to fuck you?"

"What are you doing?" Donnavin shouts when he enters the room and sees Brodie carrying Delfina to the couch.

"Who's the twerp?"

"That's Donnavin and let me go!"

Delfina says trying to squirm out of his tight hold.

"Donnavin, you've got to be kidding. Hey Shorty, if you know what's good for you, you'll leave now, before I have to fuck you up!"

Brodie put Delfina down and started to go after Donnavin, Donnavin looked at him then gave him a simple thought, and Brodie's knees buckled under him.

"Aaaah!" Brodie doubled over in pain.

"Stop, please stop it,"

"Now Brodie, you will stop giving me any shit, right!"

"Yeah yeah, just stop the pain,"

Donnavin relinquishes the pain; Brodie slowly gets to his feet,

"I'm sorry master, it was a long trip, and I guess I just got carried away,"

"Just don't let it happen again. Now come into the study, I'll give you all the information on the target. You're going to have to shadow him for a while, then do away with him."

The two men went into the other room, Delfina just sat on the couch thinking about seriously hurting Brodie. But she knew that Donnavin wouldn't have it. He probably counter act it, then punish her.

Saturday, December 19, 1981. Wayne was trying to think of an excuse to tell the guy that he was talking to on the phone.

"Well Jeff, I'll tell you what. Give me your phone number and I'll call you back later on today. Then maybe we'll be able to set something up."

Wayne wrote down the phone number, said his good-bye, and then brought Tom's coffee to him.

"Who was that?"

"Oh, just a guy I went to school with. He's been bugging me to get together with him and talk about the past."

"Well, we don't have anything to do today, if you want to go somewhere."

"I would like to drive around Dallas and Trucksville this morning to see if I'm going to pick up anything."

"We could do that, then after we finish you could take care of your social life."

"Yeah, at least this way I should be able to get him off my back. So how much will I be making?"

"They'll start you off at two hundred a week, then if you work out you'll get more."

"What's all the noise?" Anita says, bringing their attention on her. "Oh not much babe, just talking about my new job." Wayne says as he gets up to kiss his wife.

"Ton got you that job, great!"

"We're going to go driving around this morning. I'll be home sometime this afternoon."

Wayne and Tom finished their coffee, Wayne kissed his wife, and then they were off,

For the major part of the morning. Wayne and Tom were driving around, Wayne thought that he was able to sense something in Dallas, but it was too weak. He remembered the place, then went on. In the afternoon Wayne got tired of driving around, so he headed back towards Harvey's Lake. The cabins were empty and still had snow on them from the night before. He drove to the parking lot that is now empty. He remembered the child that almost drowned and was now sure that what he was doing was right.

After they finished with the lake, they headed back to Shickshinny, Tom stayed a while, then went home, Wayne called Jeff, and set up a time and place. At the Silver Top Bar three o'clock, Wayne left to go there alone, which was alright with Anita because she didn't like Jeffrey Pulp anyway.

Wayne arrived at the Silver Top Bar at 2:50 p.m. He went in and found Jeffrey Pulp on a bar stool. He walked up and sat down next to him,

"How are you doing ole buddy?"

Jeff says as soon as he sees Wayne,

"Okay Jeff, how are you doing?"

"Oh it's hanging Wayne, its hanging!"

They spent the next couple of hours talking about old classmates and what had happened to them; Jeff continued to buy Wayne's drinks. But, Wayne continued to drink his beer. He wouldn't allow himself to get drunk.

At 5:00 p.m. Jeffrey was called away by a page, he went to answer the phone. Ten minutes later he came back to finish his drink.

"I'm going to have to leave you ole buddy,"

"What's up?"

"My girlfriend just called and wants me home for dinner."

"Okay, well it was nice seeing you again."

"Yeah, perhaps we could do it again." "Perhaps."

Jeff swallowed the rest of his drink, then left. Wayne took his time with his beer, than told the bartender that he could have the rest of the drinks that were lined up in front of him. Wayne then went into the men's room to take a leak.

Wayne left the bar and went across Penn. Ave. to the Roth Co. parking lot where his car was parked. He looked up at the sign, then his mind wandered back to the time he worked there as a delivery boy. It was the Acme supermarket at that time. Then the big fire that burned it down.

It's now dark out with snow on the ground shedding some light. As he entered the parking lot he gazes around to see where he parked his car. A cold wind blew across the parking lot. Wayne pulled his jacket closer and let out a sigh. He spotted his car and started walking towards it. Then a strong impression invades his head, to get down. He dives toward the ground, and he hears it, a loud bang sound, then glass shattering. He feels something fall on his back. He rolls over to find the driver's side window of the car he was standing next to was all over his back. He got to his knees slowly and looked around, but couldn't see anything. He looked inside the car next to him and saw an old hat on the front seat. He cautiously reached in and picked it up, then grabbed a cane from the back seat. He put the hat on the cane then pushed it up fast. He heard another shot, this time he saw where the muzzle flash came from. He darted for another car in front of him. A few more shots went off. Wayne kept trying to get into a blind spot. He tried to dart for another car, but noticed that the bullets were hitting the gas tank, Wayne then jumped behind another car, when he heard a deafening explosion, which assisted him in his flight. He hit the ground hard.

It seemed as though people came out of nowhere. It was only a matter of a few minutes that a patrol car pulled up. One guy was trying to control the crowd. The other guy went near the vehicle that was burning. He heard a slight moan coming from a couple of cars away, so he went to see who it was.

"Hey Frank, call an ambulance: there's someone hurt over here," Wayne got to his feet, then fell back on a car. The patrolman went over to Wayne.

"Take it easy buddy, lay back down."

"What! What did you say?"

"I said lay back down." The patrolman said louder. Wayne just looked at him and tried to read his lips.

"I don't need to lie down, I feel alright. There was someone shooting at me from that warehouse.

More patrol cars were on scene. The fire department didn't waste time putting the fire out and foaming the area. The police managed to tactically ascend to the roof, but found nothing but empty shells from semi automatic rifle.

The ambulance took Wayne to the hospital, where he was released shortly after with most of his hearing back. After the police finished their report, they gave Wayne a ride back to his car. By this time the incident was already on the news. Wayne stopped by Tom's house on the way home to call Anita. He didn't get a chance at the hospital.

As soon as Tom saw that it was Wayne, he let him in immediately. Wayne rushed to the phone and proceeded to call. Tom knew that Anita would be upset, so he just told his wife to put some coffee on, and left Wayne alone.

"Tom, you still have connections on the police force."

Wayne said as he entered the kitchen where Tom and his wife were sitting.

"Yes, what do you need?"

"I need a rush job on a concealed weapon permit."

"Is it that bad?"

"It certainly is. I'm going to the Mall tomorrow to purchase a gun."

"I'll talk to my friends down the police station and see what I can do. Do you want me to come to the Mall with you?"

60

"Sure I could also complete my Christmas shopping. Wayne didn't stay too long; he had to get home to Anita. He instructed her to call his family to tell them that he was alright. He figured it would consume a lot of her time.

The next day Wayne, his wife, and child went to Tom's house, there they decided to go to the Mall in two cars. When they arrived at the Mall, the girls went their own way and the guys went theirs. The guys headed straight to the gun shop.

"May I help you?"

The salesman said as soon as the guys walked in.

"Yes, I need a hand gun that I could carry around with me."

"Me too."

Tom says after Wayne finished talking. Wayne turned to look at him "Well, you know that you need a special permit to carry a gun around, don't you?"

"Yes we know."

"The best defensive hand gun I could recommend, would be the Colt 45 commander,"

"Could we see it pleas" "Sure it's right here."

The salesman unlocks the gun case and pulls out a pistol, and hands it over to Wayne.

"Nice, how accurate is it?"

"It's accurate up to 25 feet. It could be custom made for more accuracy. All we have to do is put a longer barrel on it."

"How many rounds does the clip take?" "Seven."

"Well, what do you think, Tom?"

"I don't know, it looks as though this would definitely stop anyone that you wanted to stop."

"Definitely, okay I'll buy one, and I'll need a break away shoulder harness, also."

"Ditto."

"Just fill out these forms and I'll be needing a twenty five dollar deposit till I get these back from the police department. It should take a week to ten days."

"You'll call us when the permits come back?" "Yes."

They continued on with their shopping. After they finished they met up with the girls, and went to eat lunch.

"Hey Wayne, do you think your weird friend could have set you up for the shooting?"

Anita says after she puts the menu down.

"You mean Jeff? No, I doubt it. It was just a coincidence that we had met just before it happened."

"Well stranger things have happened, if you know what I mean."
"I'll keep it in mind."

Monday, December 21, 1981. Wayne and Tom went driving around all day with the police radio on. All they got was stolen Christmas packages from a car. So, they returned home,

"Wayne, you got a call from that gun shop in the Mall, They said that your gun and permit were ready," Anita said as soon as Wayne walked in the door,   "Okay, thanks hon," Wayne said as he kissed her,

"Do you think that a gun is really necessary?"
"Yes I do."
"Why can't you use that thing that you have."
"Because, when it happened, I didn't think about it. I was just trying to dodge bullets."

After Wayne ate his supper he went to pick up Tom and the two of them went to pick up their pistols.

"Can I help you gentlemen?"

A salesman asked as soon as Wayne and Tom walked in the gun shop

"Yes, we received a call today about our permits to carry concealed weapons."

Tom looked up from the display case and stated. "Wayne Homza and Tom Brinkle."

"Oh, you were the two that I waited on yesterday. You certainly must know someone, this is the fastest we ever got a permit back."

Wednesday, December 31, 1931. Wayne and Tom were kept pretty busy today. Monitoring the police band, they went along with the police on a couple of wild goose chases. Finally Wayne and Tom were on their way home at 9:00 p.m. Wayne was taking Tom to his house where Tom left his car that morning.

Wayne drove through Shickshinny then made a right down towards Shickshinny Valley. He was driving down the snow covered road, just slightly exceeding the speed limit. The snow has now been falling for an hour and the snow removal crews have not reached the road. The car was unusually quiet as they drove down the road listening to the radio. Wayne glances through the rear view mirror as he drives down the road and he sees a car rounding the corner in the distance behind him. He looks then sees it again, this time its closer, its high beams start to irritate Wayne.

"What the hell!" Wayne yells as he watches the car getting closer to him.

"What's the matter Wayne?" Tom asks just before the car passed Wayne's car.

"Ass hole!"

Wayne yells through the closed window. Then he just continued driving. Tom figured out what Wayne was complaining about.

Wayne came to the fork in the road where it didn't matter which way he went, he'd still come out at the same place. So he took a right then he saw the car blocking the bridge on the bottom of the short hill.

"Get out, quick!"

Wayne shouted to Tom, and then bent his head down. Tom opened the door then jumped out, rolled, then ran for cover, Wayne jammed the brakes on, slid his car sideways, then he heard glass in the windshield shatter. The glass in the door window started shattering next. Wayne opened his door then ran for cover. He heard more shots, then felt a burning sensation piercing the right side of his chest, he then became numb and fell to the ground clutching his chest.

The area was lit up with the falling snow and the snow that was already on the ground. Tom hit the ground after he departed from Wayne's car, and froze. He heard the shots ring out but didn't know what to do. After the shots stopped, he started remembering the Army training he had. He started low crawling towards the road with his gun drawn. Then he saw in the distance walking through the trees, what looked like a bear. He thought about going to see how Wayne was, but he knew that would be where the ambushers would be headed, to finish off what they had started. So, he crawled towards the creek away from Wayne. As both drew closer to the creek, Tom noticed that the figure was a very large man. He crawled as quietly as possible, but when he snapped a twig that was sticking up from the snow it caught Brody's attention. He turned with instinct then fired. Tom was running before Brodie fired. Tom turned and started firing at him. Brodie automatically jumped for cover, then returned the fire. Tom instantly went down and rolled down the hill into the creek. Brodie got up and walked to the hill and looked down at Tom holding his leg in pain. A smirk came to his face.

"They shoot horses, don't they?"

Came to his mind, and took his gun, then pointed it at Tom's head.

"Brodie!"

A shout came from behind Brodie. He turned to shoot, and he

heard a loud bark then felt something ripping through the center of his chest. Then there were two more before he hit the ground and rolled into the creek just below Tom's feet.

After Wayne hit the ground, he found it very hard to breathe. Every time he inhaled it would bring great pain to him. He was just able to lie there, feeling prey to anyone or anything that came along. He slowed his breathing down and put himself in a meditative trance, and willed the pain away. When he came out of the trance, he didn't know how much time had passed, but he heard gun shots just down the hill from where he was.

"Tom." He thought to himself, then got up and slowly started working his way down to where he heard the shots. There was a large man aiming his gun down at the creek. Wayne instantly took a chance and then shouted. Then he shot three rounds into the guy's chest,

Wayne didn't remember what he shouted. He just walked to the back of the creek and looked down to see the large body stagnant in its rest. Then he saw his friend Tom lying in the water. Tom looked up at him in surprise. Wayne started working his way down to Tom. He noticed the blood seeping out of his thigh.

"It looks like we were both in a mess, pal." Wayne says as he goes into the water to help Tom out. "Put your arm around my shoulder."

"What's that hissing sound?"

"I have a chest wound, we need to get to the car and wrap that litter bag that I got from Triple A, around it."

Wayne helped Tom to the top of the bank, then started ripping at his tie shirt. He ripped off three pieces. One he folded over, and placed it on Tom's wound, the next he wrapped around the folded cloth, then brought it around again and ties it right over the wound tight. Then, they continued to Wayne's car. When they reached it Wayne laid down in the back seat, putting his feet where the glass was lying, and his head on the other side of the seat. He then unzipped his jacket, and Tom folded the plastic bag that Wayne had hanging in his car, and then placed it over Wayne's wound. He then placed the third strip of his tie shirt over it and tried to wrap it around Wayne's chest twice, but it wouldn't go, so he arranged it so that the knot was over the wound.

"How we going to get some help here, Wayne. Nobody uses this road much anymore?"

"I'll call Anita." Tom looks down at Wayne. "He must be getting delirious." Tom thought to himself. He was getting very cold now.

64

That water really froze him. He started the car up and put it on full heat, even though most of the windows were broken.

Wayne was lying in the back seat shivering. Lying in the snow, then going into the water after Tom really was taking a toll on his defenses, all of the blood he lost was beginning to make him lose consciousness, but he has to hold on a little longer. He opens his eyes and stares at the ceiling of the car, then let his mind go blank. Then he searched for Anita, and locates her sitting in a chair in the parlor. Then he penetrates her thoughts now has a direct line to her.

"Anita!"

"Wayne, where are you? What's the matter?"

"I'm at the bridge just after the fork. We need help, we've been hurt."

The only thing Wayne could see now was blackness.

Anita was sitting in the parlor watching T.V. She was thinking about her husband who called and said that he was pretty busy and will be home late, probably 9 or 9:30. Then she looked up at the clock; 10:05 her thoughts changed and she was talking to her husband, "He needs my help!" She thought to herself.

First she called the State Police. She told them that her husband was five hours overdue, then gave them the route he travels. She then called the hospital and said that there was a bad accident at the place Wayne told her, he was at. After that she called Gail and asked her if she'd watch Wayne Jr., that there was a problem and she had to leave immediately. After Gail came over, Anita got into her car and took off out of the trailer park. But, by the time she reached the location that her husband was at, there were already two State Police cars there and one was stopping her from going any further. She pulled up next to the patrolman.

"You're going to have to go around the other way, miss. There's been some sort of accident here."

"I know, I think that my husband was involved."

"What's your name?"

"Anita Homza."

"Wait here please."

The officer then walked off to his car, and talked into the microphone of his radio. He put the microphone back on its slot, then walked back to Anita's car.

"They just loaded your husband in the ambulance, he's alive. You could follow it to the hospital if you want."

"Was Tom Brinkle with him?"

"Yes he was, there was also another guy."

"Is it alright if I call Mr. Brinkle's wife? It might be
better if a friend called up and told her that her husband was in an accident."

"I'll check with my superiors, but I'm sure it'll be alright,"

"Thank you."

Anita followed the ambulance to the hospital. She followed
the stretcher that her husband was on to the X—Ray room. Then
Tom was wheeled by.

"Anita, tell my wife not to worry." Tom said as he was wheeled by her.

Anita went to pay phone, and called Tom's wife. Then she was
ready to call Wayne's mother when Wayne was wheeled out of the
X-Ray room and into the elevator. A nurse walked up to her just
before she walked into the elevator.

"Mrs. Homza, I need you to sign these papers."

"What are they for?"

"They're a release. Your husband has a bullet lodged in his chest,
and the doctor has to go in immediately. This form gives us
permission to operate and remove the bullet before it does anymore
damage."

Anita took the papers, sat down on the nearest seat and started
crying. The nurse went over to try and comfort her.

"It will be alright Mrs. Homza. Your husband is a very strong
man, he'll come out of it without any problems, I'm sure."

"I know that, but what kind of future am I going to have, when I
have to worry about him every time he goes out."

".This was just a fluke, it probably won't happen again."

"It's the second time, last time he was almost killed!"

"Maybe after this time he'll quit if you talk to him."

"No, he'll never quit. He feels that he's the only one for
the job. Here's the papers giving you permission to operate. I've
gotta call his mother, thank you for talking to me, I really needed
someone to talk to"

Anita went back to the pay phone and called Wayne's mother.
She tried to break the news to his mother as soft as she could.

December 19, 1981. Brodie returned to Jeffrey Pulp's house after
he was sure that he wasn't noticed descending from the Roth Co.
roof. Donnavin had just returned himself. He had to leave Jeff's body
while Jeff was talking to Wayne. Donnavin answers the door when
Brodie knocks.

66

"Brodie, you failed. It is unlike you to fail an assignment. Perhaps I should get someone to replace you."

"No boss, I ain't one for excuses, but it seemed he knew I was going to shoot him. He ducked before I could shoot him!"

"Okay Brodie since you haven't screwed up before I will let you try again. But, if you fail this time, don't come back."

"You don't have to worry about me boss. I'm gonna tail him this time, and when the time is right, I'll blast him."

Wednesday, December 20, 1981. Brodie had followed Wayne for eleven days. He had his routine down pack. He and other members of the group kept the police busy, knowing that Wayne and his partner would also respond to the situations.

Brodie waited until Wayne was tired out from the day. That way he would be concerned with what happened, rather than what will happen.

He followed them home, keeping his distance. He was in no hurry. Wayne was going his usual route. Donnavin was heading a ceremony in one of their houses in the Heights. He was in the middle of the ceremony when he stopped.

"Our brother Brodie is dead! We will have a special mass for him."

CHAPTER VI

REVENGE BEGETS REVENGE,
ONCE IT STARTS IT WILL NEVER END.
TO STRIKE IN REVENGE AND ANGER
IS TO SWING BLINDLY AND PUT YOUSELF IN DANGER.
WHEN ANGER IS EVOKED WAIT,
OTHERWISE IT WILL BE TOO LATE.

Saturday, January 2, 1982. Delfina walks into the apartment after going to the corner store, trudging through two feet of snow for some groceries.

"Donnavin, what are we going to do about Wayne Homza? It seems as though every time we try to get him off our backs, he comes back stronger. Not to mention the fact that he is killing off our members."

"Be patient, my dear. I'm already a couple of steps ahead of him. Just remember in the game of chess, you have to lose a pawn or two, even a queen if it will put you in a position to take the king." Delfina turns to look at him.

"Yes Delfina, even you are expendable. Now first, I have to get him out of town so that I could put my plan in effect without any interruptions from him."

"What about his partner? Won't he get in the way?" "I want his partner to get in the way, without him and his friends it will be tougher for Wayne. He'll be a lone soldier in foreign lands.

Thursday, December 31. 1981. Anita stayed at the hospital all night.

The operation was a success, but Anita waited to stay near her husband.

"Mrs. Homza."

A doctor said as he entered the waiting room, waking Anita out of a light sleep.

"You don't have to stay around here, your husband is alright."

"Can I see him?"

"If you promise to go home and go to sleep afterwards."

"Okay. I promise."

"He should be sleeping till noon today; we gave him a sedative an hour ago. So, don't worry if he doesn't respond to you."

The doctor and Anita went to one of the intensive care rooms. When they entered a nurse was changing the dressing on his wound. She looked up at the doctor and Anita. The doctor gave a nod to show that it was alright to have Anita in the room. Then the nurse continued to remove the old dressing.

"Doctor, come here and look at this!"

The nurse exclaimed after she took Wayne's dressing off. The doctor walked over to Wayne's bed opposite the nurse.

"What is it nurse?"

"His wound, look at it!"

The doctor looked at the wound, and then looked up at the nurse.

"What's the matter?"

Anita asked in a worried voice.

"Oh there's nothing wrong, it's just that there is already a scar tissue on his wound and it is healing up much faster than a normal wound of this nature would take."

"Oh well, Wayne always was a quick healer. Is it all right if I sit with my husband now?"

"Sure, the nurse just has to put a new dressing on him. But, remember your promise."

"I'll so home and go to bed. All I want is a half hour with him, the nurse finished up, then both she and the doctor left the two alone.

Anita sat down in the chair next to Wayne's bed. She grabbed his hand, and then started talking to him.

"Oh Wayne, when are you going to quit so that we could have a normal life?"

A tear started coming; out of her eyes.

"I can't quit him, I love him too much!"

Anita looked over at the bed. Wayne's head was turned towards her and his hand was moving towards her face. He wiped her tear away.

"Wayne!"

Anita said and went to give him a hug.

"Wait a minute. I've got a boo boo on my chest, remember."

"I just want to hold you in my arms."

"You will tonight."

"But, the doctor said that you'll be in here at least a week."

"Did you ever hear that saying: Healer Heal Thyself?"

"Yes I have."

"What about Tom, how is hedging?"

"The doctor said that he has a broken leg."

"So then he'll be alright."

"I guess."

The doctor came in and interrupted their conversation.

"Wayne what are you doing up? You're supposed to be sleeping till this afternoon."

"I know, but I wanted to say hello to my wife. You better go home and get some sleep now hon."

"Okay."

Anita leans over his bed and gives him a kiss, then leaves. She stopped to wave to him at the door. The doctor checks Wayne over again. Then Wayne went back to sleep.

12:30 Wayne woke up, reached over for the buzzer, and rings for the nurse.

"Yes Mr. Homza, what do you need?" "Food, I'm hungry!"

"I'm sorry; you can't eat anything solid for a couple of days. Your insides have to heal up. Doctors orders, sorry." The nurse turns to walk out.

"Wait a minute! Get the doctor; I want to have a chat with him."

"I was just on my way to tell him that you're awake."

It took about ten minutes for the doctor to return with the nurse

"Good afternoon Mr. Homza. How do you feel?"

"Like I've just been shot."

The doctor walked over to him and stuck a thermometer in his mouth then started taking his pulse.

"I hear that you're hungry."

"Yes I am, I also want to get out of here."

"Oh. I'm afraid we couldn't let you do that for your own safety's sake."

"My wife signed me in, right."

"That's right."

"Well then, all you could do is suggest. My wife will be signing me out as soon as she gets down here."

"But Wayne, other complications could develop. We need to keep you under observation in case something unforeseen happens."

"I'm sorry Doc, I've got things to do, and one of them is not lying in this bed."

The doctor noticed that Wayne's vital signs were all normal.

"You seem to be getting well faster than normal. But, there still could be something hidden, an infection, or something else internal that isn't showing up now."

"I'm going to have to take that chance. For now could you please take this I.V. out of my arm?"

Anita arrived at the hospital at 2:30 with Jean Brinkle. Wayne was able to talk the doctor into removing the I.V. As soon as Anita entered Wayne's room, he sent her back out again to sign him out of the hospital. When she returned, Wayne was dressed in the clothes that she brought him.

A nurse followed her in with a wheelchair.

"I won't be needing a wheel chair,"

"I realize that, but its hospital policy."

"Okay, but would you take me to Mr. Brinkle's room please?"

"Sure, he's been asking for you,"

The nurse wheeled Wayne into Tom's room.

"Hey bum, how are you doing?" Wayne asked as soon as he entered Tom Brinkle's room.

"I'd be doing a lot better if I didn't have this cement boot on. You look as cheerful as always."

"It's these vitamins that they give you in these hospitals."

"Hey Wayne, come here."

Wayne wheeled himself close to Tom. Tom whispered to him.

"How about fixing my leg so that I could leave the hospital also?"

"I'm sorry buddy, but I think that you will be safer in here."

"The cops say that the guy was a hit man for the Mafia. He was probably after me anyway."

"I don't think so, anyway that group is planning something and I don't know what it is. I feel that they will try to come after you some way."

"Well if that is so, then I want to be able to get them, and I won't be able to if I'm laid up."

"Good point. I'll advance your healing process a little Bit. Nurse could I borrow your pen?"

"Sure here."

Wayne took the pen from her, then went to Tom's leg and started writing something. While he was writing he was concentrating on the bones mending together.

Monday, January 4, 1982. Wayne reported in for work, and he was immediately told to go to the general manager's office. When he entered the office he noticed that the news director was in there also.

"Come in Wayne, have a seat." Wayne entered the large office and sat down.

"How are you feeling today, Wayne?"

"I'm feeling alright Mr. Roberts. How are you feeling?"

"Oh, I'm doing alright. We called you in here to let you know that you're doing a very good job and we would like to send you on an assignment to LA., if you'd want to go."

"What type of assignment is it?"

"There is an occult group out there that's really making trouble, and with your past experience on the subject, and seeing that Tom Brinkle will be laid up for a couple of weeks, you seem to be the right person for the job."

"Okay, when do I leave?"

"This afternoon, we'll reserve a ticket for you at the airport. It will be on TWA and will leave at three o'clock."

"I'll be there."

Wayne went to the hospital to visit Tom after he left the General Manager's office. He told him that he was selected to go Los Angeles. Tom was glad for him. Wayne thought that Tom would be jealous. He then put the final touches on Tom's leg then went home to tell his wife. She wasn't as acceptable to the idea as Tom was.

Wayne, Anita, and Wayne Jr. were at the Wilkes-Barre Airport at 2:4-5 p.m. Wayne kissed Anita good-bye. Then boarded the plane.

Wayne tried to sleep most of the trip. But, he had to get off the plane in Chicago. When the plane started its approach to LA., all Wayne could see now was mountains, and then all of a sudden the airport came in view.

After Wayne left the plane, he piled up his bags, then went to the information counter. But instead of seeing the reporter that was supposed to help him, he received a note from the lady behind the counter:

MR. HOMZA, SORRY BUT I AM DELAYED AT THE STATION. THERE IS A CAR RESERVED FOR YOU AT THE HERTZ RENT A CAR STATION. GET ON TO CENTURY EAST FOLLOW IT TO HARBOR FREEWAY. TAKE IT NORTH TO SANTA MONICA FREEWAY, GO EAST UNTIL YOU HIT THE INTER CHANGE, TAKE IT NORTH UNTIL YOU GET TO THE BONAVENTURE HOTEL. YOU WILL HAVE A ROOM WAITING FOR YOU THERE. I WILL CALL YOU WHEN I GET FREE. SORRY AGAIN.

JIM HAYES

Wayne looked at his watch; it was now seven o'clock, and dark out. He went to pick up his car, and then followed the directions on the paper that's on the seat next to him. It didn't take too long for Wayne to reach his destination; he just caught the tail end of the rush hour traffic.

Wayne checked into his room, and was surprised at how expensive the
hotel looked to him. As soon as he got to his room, he lay down on his bed, and then his phone rang,

"Wayne Homza?" "Yes."

"Hi, this is Jim Haynes, I see that you found the hotel alright.

"Yes, I didn't have any real problem."

"How about if we meet for dinner?"

"Okay, where?"

"The restaurant in the Bonaventure is a very good one,"

"Okay, give me a chance to shower and get dressed,"

"Does eight o'clock sound alright?"

"Sure, see you then,"

"I'll reserve a table for us,"

"Okay bye."

"Bye,"

Wayne took a shower, put his clothes away, then went down to the restaurant.

"Table for one?"

The hostess asked when Wayne walked up to her.

"No. a Mr. Hayes reserved a table."

"Wait a minute, I'll check. Oh yes here it is. Mr. Hayes has not showed up yet."

"Alright, can you show me to the table please?"

"It's right over here."

Wayne followed her to a table in the back away from everything. Then the hostess gave him a menu and put one opposite him. Wayne just looked at the prices of the food, and was glad that ABC was reimbursing him for this trip.

Fifteen minutes later, Wayne noticed the hostess leading a man over to his table. The man was six foot and stocky. He looked like he should have been a defensive line man for the Pittsburg Steelers.

"Wayne Homza, I'm Jim Hayes. How do you do?" The guy said as he approached the table. He reached his hand out.

"I'm doing fine."

Wayne says as he takes Jim's hand with a firm grip and shakes it.

"Did you order yet?"

"No, I was waiting for you to show up."

"Well lets order."

The two men ordered their dinner, and ate it without much discussion. Mainly small talk about the weather. They waited until they were finished eating their dinner before they started talking business.

"Do you know exactly why you're out here?"

"Recently the occult has been very active. But we could not point the finger at them because we couldn't get any type of proof. Within the last week alone fifteen teenagers have disappeared from different

74

parts of the town. There have only been three that showed up,"

"Where did they find the three?"

"One drove his car into the ocean, another one was found by a motorist when he stopped to take a piss, it was a hit and run. The third one was found in Kalibu Canyon. She was cut in different pieces, and spread around. They still didn't find her heart. The Wilkes-Barre office said that you were very good at this kind of thing. So, I hope you could shine some light on the subject,"

"Well, I'll do my best."

"Now would you like to meet some hookers, or go bar hopping?"

"No thanks, I'm happily married, and I hardly drink. But, I would like to read the police reports on the missing teenagers."

"You are all work and no play aren't you? Okay, I've got a copy of the reports in my briefcase. But it will take you all night to read them."

"That's okay, I have all night."

Jim gave the reports to Wayne. He took them up to his room and started reading them. He touched each picture, but couldn't receive anything. It was like there was a cloud or a film covering the pictures that stopped him from reading them.

Friday, January 8, 1982. Tom Brinkle was out of the hospital and walking without crutches. He still had a limp but he was able to put his full weight on it. While Tom was in the hospital things started acting up around Wilkes-Barre. Tom went right to work on it. He went to Dallas, PA. and drove around other places that Wayne had a feeling about. But, he couldn't find anything. He went to the farms in the area and asked the farmers about missing livestock, but still had no luck. Then one day he noticed that he was being followed. While he was watching the car through his rear view mirror, he was reaching into his holster, then he chambered around in his gun. Then he stepped on the gas, the car behind him also sped up. He led them to a dead end street in Forty Fort. He stopped and got out, one carrying a pipe, and the other carrying a chain. Tom pulled his gun out of his holster.

"Alright guys hold it right there!" Tom said in a stern voice.

"Now wait a minute there's no need for that, there's been some kind of mistake."

The driver said with a shaky voice.

"There sure has been, and you two just made it. Now both of you get into your car and I want to see your hands on the dash and on the steering wheel,"

Tom aimed the gun at them then he shot off two rounds, one in the front driver's side tire, and the other one in the rear driver's side tire. Then he walked up to the driver's side window aiming his gun at the driver's head.

"Now you tell your boss that next time the holes will be in your head instead of in the tires."

Tom then got back into his car and drove off before the cops got there.

A couple of hours later the two guys reported what had happened to Donnavin.

"More of Wayne Homza rubbed off on to Brinkle than I thought. Well, I'll have to plan something more in depth. Fortunately, our friends on LOS Angeles are keeping Wayne busy, because this is going to take some time," Donnavin said to Delfina.

Tuesday, January 5-1982. Wayne got up at seven o'clock, and went downstairs for breakfast. Jim showed up at Wayne's table at eight o'clock.

"Good morning, Wayne,"

"Mornin Jim, pull up a chair and have a cup of coffee."

"No thanks I don't drink coffee,"

"You don't drink coffee! That's un-American," Wayne said with a smile to let Jim know that he was joking,

"Well Jim, where are we going to go from here?" Wayne said after he finished eating.

"Well first go to Malibu Canyon, then I'll take you to Topanga Canyon, Maybe we'll be able to find something at those places."

"Okay, I'm ready to go."

Both of them went in Jim's car. They went to Malibu Canyon first, Wayne was looking at the cliffs at the edge of the roadway. He looked down and saw an old wreckage from an unknown person speeding around the corner.

"Why aren't there guard rails in some places?"

"The city hasn't gotten around to putting them there yet,"

"Boy, that looks dangerous!"

"I know, our station did a special on it once, but it did no good." They went, down to where the girl was found. The area was marked off for police investigation.

"They already filed this case, they just didn't, get around to taking down the ropes yet." Jim said as he bent over and went under the ropes. Wayne followed. When they got to the crime scene. Wayne let his mind go blank and started feeling around the dirt with his hands.

Then he found the spot that was generating emotions. Pictures started forming in his mind. Then he became an observer.

A girl about fourteen was walking home after school. She had a small pile of books pushed against her breast. She was joking around with her best friend. They were talking about boys. Patty, is her name. She looks across the street to see the same car that she had seen parked many times in different places for a week now. She turns the same corner that she turns every day, and continues to walk, and to try to make her friend blush. Then she hears someone yell to her.

"Hey can you tell me where Brooke street is?" She and her girlfriend look over and see the same car that Patty saw for the last week. There are two guys in the front and the one on the passenger side of the car was trying to get directions from them. She totally ignored everything the school was trying to teach her about walking up to stranger's cars. They taught her to give directions from a distance, and if they did try something, to write their license plate number on the sidewalk or something, then report it to the police. But, she trusted people, there's no reason that anyone would want to hurt her, besides he didn't talk loud enough.

"What street was that?"

Patty said as she got closer to the car. Her girlfriend was just a couple of inches behind her and to the left.

"Get in the car and don't say a word or I'll have to shoot you." The guy in the passenger seat said with a stern voice, while he pointed the gun at Patty. Her girlfriend looked at the gun, screamed and started running away from the car. The guy aimed the gun and shot her in the back. She was dead before she hit the ground.

"Shit!"

The guy yelled as he got out of the car. He grabbed Patty, and threw her into the back seat of the car. Patty watching it all just froze. The voices were in a distance.   "Give me the trunk keys." The passenger yelled. He opened the trunk, then picked the dead girl up, like a rag doll, then threw her into the trunk. Patty heard the thump, and that sound of her best friend landing in the trunk stayed with her.

They drove off and ended up at Topanga Canyon. The passenger got out again with the trunk keys. He opened the trunk and the smell of the girl's bowel movements hit him in the face. He found some old army fold up shovels and got one out, then dug a hole. After he finished he threw the dead girl in it then buried her. Then they continued on. Wayne could see them get on the Hollywood freeway, but he can't tell where they went from there. The girl in the car blacked out.

After a while his vision started fading out, but he could see the car again. Then he looked at the large houses near the car. They were mansions. They made him think of "Dark Shadows", a soap opera that he used to watch when he was way younger. Then he saw Patty lying on the back seat of the car. Her girlfriend's spirit followed her. Now she's looking at Wayne, and trying to talk to him. There were no words coming from her mouth, but she was still trying to tell Wayne something. Then the words became clear to him: Hancock Park.

Jim Hayes was walking around the inside of the roped off area, looking around. He would once an a while glance at Wayne, and not think anything of him just staying in one place. But, after a half an hour he started to get worried. He walked over to Wayne.

"Wayne, are you alright?" No answer.

"Wayne! Hey Wayne, don't "be kidding around now!" Jim went over and started shaking Wayne and calling his name. But there was no answer, Jim was scared, he started towards his car to call for help on the CB radio then he heard Wayne let out a breath, Jim walked back to Wayne,

"Wayne, are you alright?"

"Sure, why what's up?" Wayne said   catching his breath,

"What's up!   You had me scared to death!   What the fuck were you doing?"

"Trying to find something out. Do you know of a Hancock Park?"

"Where did you hear about Hancock Park? Are you some kind of psychic or something?"

"Or something, look the only way we could get anything done is by working with each other, and not telling anyone about me,"

"It's your talent, if you want to keep it a secret it's alright by me, Hancock Park is a place where there's a lot of mansions. What about it?

"That's where this girl was taken. Her girlfriend was buried at Topanga Canyon. Let's go there and I'll show you the grave site."

They drove to Topanga Canyon, it looked a lot like Malibu Canyon, When Wayne started to notice the area, he started pointing out where to go. They finally ended up at the grave site.

"Do you think we should call the police now?" Jim asked.

"No, lets first make sure she's here, we don't want any egg on our faces." Wayne walked up to the place he saw in his vision, then started digging with his hands. It took him a little while, but he uncovered a hand. Now a light drizzle started to fall, Wayne looked up and noticed that the sun had hidden behind some gray clouds,

"You could call the police now,"

Jim walked over, saw the hand, and walked back to his car, turned his C.B. radio on channel nine then called them. Wayne looked and saw Patty and her girlfriend together again. They both looked very content,

"Thank you." They said in unison, then disappeared, After the police came and both Wayne and Jim said that they uncovered the body accidently, they got on the Hollywood freeway and headed towards Hancock Park, Now the drizzle turned to a down pour, and the wind was picking up quite a bit. It got so bad, that Jim could only drive ten miles per hour. By mutual agreement they went back to the Bonaventure Hotel. Jim went up to Wayne's room, he sensed that something was wrong, he put the key in the lock and opened the door entering quickly. When he entered he turned the lights on, and wasn't surprised at what he saw. The place was a wreck, furniture was turned over, lamps and vases were smashed, Jim looked at his apartment,

"Who did this?"

"My friends, the ones that killed them two girls."

"Nice friends, are you going to call the cops?"

"I have to otherwise they charge this damage to ABC,"

"How did they find you so soon?"

"Either someone at your station talked, or they tuned in on me." Wayne said as he walked into the bathroom. He noticed that written on the mirror was: BARRA!   MASKIK XUL.

"Wayne, your phone is dead." Jim said as he enters the bathroom.

"What the hell is that?"

"It's a warning from our friends."

"What does it say?"

"It says Begone! Evil Fiend. (Ambusher, Lier-in-wait.) "What's it mean?"

"It means that they're going to get in touch with them evil gods, and use them against me."

"Could they do it?"

"Yes, they've tried before. If I'm not on my toes, they could succeed,"

"What about me?"

"Oh, they will certainly go after you too. If you want to pull out do it now before they start to go after you first."

"No, I'm going to see this one through. If you want you could stay with me and my wife."

"No thanks, that would attract them to your house. I'll stay here. Let's go find someone that has a phone and call the desk about this."

"Okay, what is that stuff that those words are written in?"

"It looks like dried up blood."

They went across the hall and knocked on the door.

"Just a minute," a voice came from inside. "Yes, can I help you?" A beautiful woman says as she answers the door in a black evening dress with a slit on the side that goes up past her thigh,

"My name is Jim Hayes and this is Wayne Homza, we're with channel two. We'd like to know if we could use your phone, we had a little trouble with my friend's room."

The lady looked at the I.D, that Jim was showing her.

"Okay, but I'm going to be going out soon, so make it quick." As Wayne entered her apartment, he was able to see through her disguise. She had what was called a sugar daddy. A guy to pay for her pad, and yet come back whenever he told his wife he had to work late. Wayne saw that this could work out for him. He picked up the phone which was a direct line to the desk.

"Front Desk, may I help you?"

"Yes, this is Wayne Homza in room 730, and I need to see the manager. My room was broken into and everything was vandalized."

"I'll tell him, and he'11 be up immediately," Wayne hung up the phone then turns towards the lady. "Do you think that the judge could get me a permit to carry a concealed weapon here in Los Angeles?"

"What! I don't know what you're talking about!"

"Look miss, I don't have time to play games, I know that a prominent judge is paying the rent on this place, I also know that my life could be in danger in the near future and that I will need to carry my gun around legally. I have a permit, but it's for Pennsylvania."

"I don't know, I don't like asking him for many favors."

"All I ask, is that you try."

"Okay, I'll try, you won't tell anyone about Me , will you?"

No, I have no intention to do that. The cops will probably ask you if you heard anything, though.

Wednesday, January 6, 1982, Wayne spent most of the day running around the town trying to get a permit to carry his gun around concealed, in the afternoon he finally got it. The judge came through for him,

Jim and Wayne were kept pretty busy for a couple of days chasing down reports of occult meetings and places children are seen going in, But never coming out. Most were crank calls to the police, and ended up being child care centers to bingo patrons. Every time they tried to go to Hancock Park, another call would come in and they would respond to it,

Sunday, January 10. 1982, Wayne and Jim finally got a chance to visit Hancock Park. They decided that they weren't going to answer any more calls on the scanner.

At ten o'clock in the morning, they left the Bonaventure Hotel in Jim's car so that they'd be able to listen to the scanner. They got on the Hollywood freeway and followed it down to the exit that brought them to Hancock Park, Once entering; Wayne opened himself up for anything that would be in the air. His mind was probing the mansions that just sat staring at them as they drove by. Then Wayne looked and knew that the house ahead of them was the one that the occult group was housed in,

"See that house up there?" Wayne said pointing to a house up on the left side of the road.

"Is that it?"

"Yes, pull over here; we'll walk the rest of the way,"

Jim pulled his car over and the two got out and started walking towards the house. When they started getting closer, Wayne closed himself off mentally. He didn't want to give them any early warnings. They walked past the house and turned to look up at the windows to see what they could see but, the windows were painted black. So, they turned around and walked back. Jim went up to the front door, while Wayne ran around the back of the house.

Jim knocked on the door, but there was no answer. He knocked loudly, then put his ear up to the door to listen for footsteps, but he heard none. He left the porch to go around to where Wayne was. It was a long walk, but Jim finally caught up with Wayne, Wayne was trying to look in the basement windows, but they also were painted black, also.

"Nobody answers the door. Is there a way for you to find out if there is anyone home?"

"There is but if someone is home, it will be like using a bull horn telling them that were here."

"So what do we do?" "We break in."

"They've got dead bolts on the door."

"Yes, but not on the windows."

Wayne went to the very back of the house where he couldn't be seen by anyone. He then went up to a window, pulled the bottom of the screen out which made it bend at the middle. That enabled him to unhook the screen. He then pulled out a pen knife and put the point of it to where he thought the latch should be located. Then he pushed it to the frame which made the aluminum bend out. Then he did the same thing to the other side.

"Storm windows are the easiest. Do you have a knife on you?" Wayne said to Jim. Jim pulled out a knife and handed it to Wayne.

"Put it in on that latch, you've got to push it so that the window will come up."

They get the window all the way up, then crawled through it. They got inside on the first floor. It is pitch black and they could hardly see five inches in front of them,

"Which way do we go?" Jim whispered,

"No way! You wait until our eyes get accustomed to the darkness"   The two of them just stood in the one spot for fifteen minutes.

"How long do we have to wait?" Jim asked,

"It takes thirty minutes for your eyes to get fully adjusted to the darkness. But, I guess we could start moving now."

Wayne started walking and Jim stayed right behind him. The house was old and once in a while the floors would creek. There was a damp musty odor in the air. Wayne stopped short when he heard a noise coming from the basement, Jim bumps into him, Wayne looked and saw the outline of the staircase. He headed towards it, then he ascends it with Jim close behind. When they reached the top, they could hear the voices getting louder, they were female voices.

"I don't think that he should have had the electricity turned off until we were totally moved out," One girl said to the other,

"I know, it's very dark in here. At least before we had an option to turn the lights on"

"I wonder how the boys are doing in the attic?"

"Let's go find out,"

Wayne looked down the stairway and could see two beams of light going towards the steps. Then he started backing up and by instinct turned quickly, he knew someone was behind him but it wasn't Jim, He was on the other side of the staircase. He put his hands up in an X, and caught something on his wrists, a large metal flashlight. He then grabbed it, pulled it towards him, then kicked

82

what was in front of him in the groin, then did a side kick in the stomach, he heard a body hit the wall, so he side stepped and the body hit the floor beside him.

Wayne still had the flashlight in his hands; he turned it on and shined it at Jim. Right beside him was a guy with a bar getting ready to swing it at Jim's head. Jim saw him, ducked, then tackled him and started throwing punches at his face. The girl heard the noise and went running up the stairs. Wayne saw them; he pulled out his gun and pointed it at them, "Freeze!" Wayne shouted. The girls stopped and looked at the gun that Wayne made sure they could see by shining the light on it,

"Who are you? What do you want?" One of the girls asked Wayne.

"It doesn't matter who I am. I want your leader!"

Wayne said watching Jim drag the other guy out in the open. The girls just looked at him then the sounds of the guy that Wayne took care of started penetrating the still air. His breath was short and was snorting loudly, "Will that guy live?" Jim asked,

"Unfortunately yes, I just knocked the air out of him." Wayne looked around with the flashlight,

"Pick up the flashlight that the guy had, and see if you could find a bedroom with some furniture in it."

"Okay Wayne, watch these guys. Especially the women, you can't really trust them."

Jim went off and came back in five minutes,

"There's a bedroom down here Wayne it's got everything in it."

"Good, take these guys down there and tie them up, I'll wait for you here and make sure these two don't go anywhere,"

Jim carried one guy down to the bedroom, then came back for the second one.

"You're Wayne Homza, aren't you?" One of the girls asked Wayne.

"Yes I am, so you have been expecting me?"

"Yes, but not this soon. Look why don't you join our group, it's the only thing you can do to save your life."

"No, I could save my life by not joining this group."

"Okay Wayne, they're tied up now what?"

"Now we take these two down there and wait for their leader to find out what had happened to them."

Wayne and Jim waited in the bedroom for an hour and a half, taking insults from their captives. Then finally they heard keys entering the lock of the front door. Then Wayne felt a strong probe of the area. He could hide his own feeling and emotions, but his captives gave him away. Wayne heard a loud yell in his mind. He couldn't hide it anymore; he had to release protection for himself and Jim.

All of a sudden, the windows and doors opened up. The sunlight temporarily blinded everyone in the room. Wayne got up and ran out of the bedroom to meet his foe.

"Stay in here Jim and watch them."

Wayne shouted as he ran out the door. He got to the top of the stairs and looked down at a man in his thirties, same height as Wayne, and almost as stocky as Wayne.

"Wayne this is the end of your career!"

"I'm sorry; I have no plans for an early retirement. I don't understand what you feel that you're going to gain out of this."

"The satisfaction knowing that I destroyed the guy that destroyed our leader."

"If you say so, give it your best shot." Then all of the doors on the second floor closed. Wayne

could hear Jim run to the door and try the doorknob. Wayne looked over at his foe and started to see more than one face show up. He felt a bitter coldness in the air; icicles started forming off the wall lamps. "I know he can't be responsible for all this," Wayne thought to himself. Then he started to wonder into

the past. All the sacrifices and screaming's were flashing in his mind. Then the guy in front of him pulled out a gun but Wayne had his out first, he was too dizzy, he wasn't sure of his target. He did a shoulder roll, and heard a loud blast. That shook him out of it. He aimed and fired the bullet hitting the guy in the wrists, which made his gun fire then drop to the floor,

Wayne could feel different entities trying to enter his body; He leaped and gave the guy in front of him a side kick in the chest. The guy went against the wall then fell to the floor. Wayne heard a lot of banging sounds coming from the bedroom that Jim was in. He picked the gun off the floor, emptied it out, and threw it away. Then he started towards the bedroom when he was jumped from behind, and wrestled to the floor. The guy was starting to get the best of Wayne when he rolled over and gave him a chop in the Adams apple. Wayne got up with that guy choking and rolling around on the floor. Wayne just reached the bedroom door when he was torn away with inhuman strength, and was thrown against the wall. Wayne hit the wall bounced off, rolled to his feet. The same guy was on top of him that fast. Wayne moved out of his way just in time, he pulled his gun out and shot him in the chest just before he reached Wayne, The guy immediately fell to the floor. Wayne used his mind to spring the bedroom door open. All four of the people inside were attacking Jim. Jim would throw them across the room but they'd return as though they weren't injured at all. Wayne rushed in and started flipping them out the window. He did it until no one was left in the room.

"Come on Jim, let's get the hell out of here fast!"

Then Wayne stopped short in his tracks. That guy was standing in the doorway. A small hole in the center of his chest where blood was trickling out, but on the back side of him there was hardly any spine left just a very large hole caused by the bullet. Wayne looked at Jim, he was in bad shape. Wayne didn't feel like getting into a physical fight with the guy, he knew that he'd lose, Wayne sent out a mental charge that flushed out three different entities, then the body fell to the floor. Both Wayne and Jim left that place as fast as they could. When Wayne reached the front door he mentally opened it. Outside the other four people started walking towards the front with broken legs and all, Wayne and Jim just ran to the car and left in a hurry.

Saturday, January 30, 1982. Without Wayne, Tom Brinkle didn't have much luck locating anything that had to do with the group. Although once he found a grave dug up in the Forty Fort cemetery. This particular day Tom had a lot of missing persons calls. And visited the house that reported it to the police. Most of them were kids that didn't get home in the scheduled time. But finally made it home. There were a few still missing.

At Jeffrey pulp's house Donnavin and Delfina were making the final plans for the day. Then they left and went to the house in the Heights.

At 11:15 a car left the house in the Heights. A half an hour later they arrived at Tom Brinkle's house, a girl and a guy got out, and walked on to the porch. The girl rang the doorbell while the guy stepped to one side. Jean Brinkle came to the door.

"Yes, can I help you?"

"I'm your neighborhood Avon lady and would like to show you our product."

"No thank you. I have enough cosmetics."

"The lady said that she wants to show you her product!"

The guy popped out with a gun, and said with his teeth closed and his lips moving,

"Don't make a sound, or else you're a dead lady,"

"What do you want? I don't have much money,"

"Just open the door,"

As soon as Jean opened the door, the two entered, and then another guy came up from the car and entered the house,

"Tommy, run!"

Jean shouted to one of their sons. The first guy took the butt of his pistol and hit her with it on the back of the head, Jean fell to the ground. Tommy just started running for the back door, but when he reached it, it was locked. He fumbled with the lock, but by the time he got it unlocked the girl was on top of him and grabbed him. She picked him up and carried him back to the living room.

"Let me take care of the kid," The girl said to one of the guys.

"Fine, we'll take care of the mommy here," The girl carried the little boy up stairs to a bedroom. He was kicking and crying all the way.

The two guys picked Jean up and put her on the couch. One guy went to get some water, then threw it on Jean's face, in an attempt to revive her. After a while, she finally came to.   "Where's your little girl?"

One guy asked. Jean looked around and it finally came to her what had happened.

"She's out playing somewhere." Slap. The guy gave her a back hand.

"Now let's try it again, where's your little girl?"

"I don't know, she's out playing somewhere," Slap... The guy gave her another back hand. Jean was now crying, her face was beet red. She got up and tried to run, but she wasn't quick enough. The guys tackled her, hit her some more then threw her back on the couch.

"What do you want?"

Jean said with tears streaming down her face, and her mouth in an awkward shape.

"We want your little girl; we want to bust her cherry."

"Oh please no, leave her alone, she hasn't done anything to you!"

The two guys tried every way that they could to get the information out of Jean. But, a mother's love and protectiveness for her child cannot be broken by physical means.

2:30 p.m. Tom got tired of running around, so he decided to stop by his house to apologize to his wife. Lately he has been on edge from putting in too much time at work. So, he snapped at her when she asked when he was going to be home. Tom pulled up in his driveway, got out of his car and went onto his porch. He put the key into the keyhole, turned it then pushed the door. He noticed that the dead bolt was locked. He gave it an inquisitive look, then unlocked the dead bolt and opened the door. He looked inside and all he saw was a blur of bodies run across the floor to the back door. He instinctively pulled at his gun, and started to chase after them, until he saw a body on the floor, this one was familiar to him.

"Oh God! Jean!"

He ran to her side and put her bloodied head on his lap. "Jean, what happened?" He said with tears in his eyes.

"Tommy, where's Tommy?"

Jean said barely conscious. Then Tom heard a muffled scream come from upstairs. He let Jean's head down gently, then bolted up the stairs, He went to the bedroom where he heard the scream come from. Then he busted in the door. The girl was standing over little Tommy's limp body. Unaware of what was going on down stairs. Tom aimed his gun, and all he heard from the girl was "NO!" Then he emptied his gun into her body.

A neighbor heard the gun shots and called the police, then went over to see what was going on. Tom returned downstairs with Tommy in his arms. He put him on the couch. He picked Jean up into his arms. At that time the neighbor showed up at the door.

"Get an ambulance!" Tom shouted trying to keep his sanity. "Where's Shari?" Jean asked. Tom's mind went looking, then he remembered his daughter was unaccounted for.

"Shari!" Tom bellowed. The neighbor had just gotten off the phone with the local ambulance company.

"She's over my house Tom, she's alright. I'll watch her for you till you or your wife gets back from the hospital.

Saturday, January 30, 1982. Wayne had decided that he wasn't needed in Los Angeles anymore. The disappearances have decreased greatly since the night that Wayne and Jim visited Hancock Park. But, Jim wouldn't let Wayne leave without a party for him. Wayne checked out of the apartment and went over to Jim's house. Right after Wayne left he got a person-to person call from Tom Brinkle. Since Wayne didn't want to be bothered he didn't leave any forwarding address or phone number. When he got at Jim's house, Wayne noticed that Jim's phone was taken off the hook.

"I don't want anyone to bother us while we're partying." Jim said before Wayne had a chance to say anything about it, Wayne just let himself go at this party. He drank until he was feeling good and didn't worry about anything. He stayed at Jim's until the first of February; he wanted to surprise his wife so he didn't tell her that he was coming home.

The ambulance arrived at Tom's house shortly after the neighbor made the call. The attendants could not pronounce the boy dead because they didn't have a doctor. They rushed both Jean and Tom Jr. to the hospital where the doctor pronounced Tom Jr. D. 0 A. His mother died shortly after.

The doctor had to sedate Tom. But, through his drowsiness he still was able to call Wayne's hotel in LA. He felt as though Wayne was the only one that could help him now. He was sure that Wayne would be able to wake his wife up from her uncertain sleep. But when he found out that Wayne checked out, he lost it. He had to be admitted to the hospital.

February 1, 1982. Early in the morning Tom and his daughter, Sheri buried his wife and son. He then had his neighbor babysit for Sheri while he took the elevator of the United Perm Bank building to the top floor. Then he got on the roof, walked over to the edge, looked down with tears flowing out of his eyes. He thought of Jean, and little Tommy, all he wanted to do was follow them into the next world. He got up on the ledge and gets ready to jump,

Wayne landed at the Avoca airport early in the afternoon. He had to leave early in order to arrive in Wilkes-Barre early in the afternoon. He caught a limousine service sign and inquired about the price. He found that it would be cheaper to take a limousine than it would be to take a cab. So, he decided to take one to his mother's house. Unlike cabs, these limousines have commercial radios in them.

"Boy I tell you, this city wasn't safe to live in anymore." The driver said trying to strike up a conversation.

"Why do you say that?" Wayne asked, knowing that he had to come back with something.

"Where have you been these last couple of days?"

"Los Angeles."

"Oh, that explains it. A couple of days ago someone broke into a guy's home and killed his wife and boy. For no reason at all, they just went inside and beat them to death."

"Oh yeah, whose house was that?"

The driver was just about ready to answer when something on the radio caught his interest.

"This is the guy, listen." The driver then turned the radio up.

"I repeat, stay away from the United Penn building on Franklin and Market streets. You will only make things worse, close friends and relatives of Tom Brinkle have already been notified."

"Turn it to another station please, and head downtown fast." The driver turned the station until found one that had the news on it.

"They just said not to go downtown."

"I know that, but I'm that guy's best friend, I've got to find out what's going on."

"There is a man on the roof of the United Penn building and it looks like he's ready to jump off. The police are up there now trying to talk him out of it. So please don't go down there you will only make things worse,"

"Was that the guy that lost his wife and little boy?"

"It sure was, I'd probably be trying suicide if that had happened to me."

"Maybe, but if I can help it, than it won't happen. Can't we go any faster?"

"I'm going as fast as I can. Oh, look at this traffic jam."

"Go down Penn. Ave, and turn on Market,"

"Okay mister, it's your money. To Wayne's amazement there wasn't much traffic on Penn Ave, But, when they got a block away from Market street, there weren't any cars moving, Wayne got out, handed the driver a twenty, then sprinted off. He had to get off the sidewalk because of the mess of people just in his way. He started running between the cars, but it was too slow, so he leaped up on the trunk of one car and went from one car to another until he was able to get close enough to the United Penn building, Wayne looked up and tried to yell out to his friend. Then all of a sudden he saw the figure on the roof jump. There were screams all around him, he concentrated hard, and then the figure just froze where it was. From the bottom it just looked like the figure was leaning over.

Wayne pushed his way through the crowd and tried to enter the building, but a cop stopped him, Wayne then pulled out his press card and explained that he was Tom's friend. The cop hesitated so Wayne pushed his way into the building. He ran to the elevator, and pushed for the top floor. It seemed to take forever, for the elevator to reach the top. As soon as it did Wayne ran out and bolted for the stairs that led to the roof.

There were more policemen by the door, and they were ready to grab Wayne. Wayne didn't have any time for them; he just used telekinesis to push them out of the way. When Wayne did that to the guards, it moved Tom a little. Wayne made it to the roof where the policeman stopped him and pushed him back. He just broke away from them and ran over to Tom. He knew that Tom wasn't going anywhere. He used his powers to lift Tom up all the way and set him on the ledge. He knew that he could stop Tom from jumping but couldn't stop the problems by physically restraining him from jumping. Wayne looked in Tom's eyes but only saw a blank expression. Tom's mind was elsewhere.

"Tom, Tom, its Wayne come on down, let's talk about it," Wayne not only verbally talked to Tom, but he mentally talked to him at the same time. He broke through the wall that Tom built around himself. Tom looked down at Wayne, and then returned from the blank expression.

"Wayne!, where were you when I needed you? You could have helped me. You could have saved their lives, but you weren't here. You killed them!"

Tom took a swing at Wayne, but missed. He lost his balance swirled around like a drunk that lost his balance. Wayne just caught his shirt, went with the momentum, and pulled him onto the roof gently. Tom just collapsed into a fountain of tears. Rattling on how he hates Wayne and that Wayne could have saved his family. Wayne's mind wandered back to when the orderly told him that Phyllis had just died. He remembered the pain, and that he couldn't see past his emptiness.

Wayne put his arm around Tom and helped him walk across the roof to the stairway. The ambulance attendant then took over, they shot him up with something that knocked him right out. A couple of his relatives just showed up, and then Anita came up after them.

"Wayne!, when did you get here?" Anita asked with a surprised look on her face.

"I just got here hon!"

"We all have been trying to get in touch with you for the past two days. We buried Jean and Tommy this morning."

"Anita, don't make me feel any worse than I already feel. You know that if I knew what had happened, that I would have been here already. Come on, you drive, let's go to the hospital where they're taking him. Then I want you to tell me what had happened on the way."

Wayne said while they were on the elevator on the way down.

At the hospital, Tom woke out of his drug induced sleep, and asked for Wayne. Wayne was more than happy to go into Tom's room. As he walked in, the doctor told him not to stay too long, because Tom needed the rest.

"Wayne, come in!" Tom said with tear filled eyes.

"I want to apologize for what I said up there."

"It's alright Tom you don't have to. If I were in the same situation I might have done the same thing."

"No Wayne, not you. You're much too strong for that. I don't know what came over me, it was like I was possessed."

"It was grief Tom."

Wayne understands the minds workings a lot better now, and he knows that a little more is involved than just grief taking over Tom's body.

"The main reason I called you in here is Shari."

"Shari."

"Yes, I want you and Anita to watch over her while I'm here."

"Sure, we'll be glad to watch over her. You just relax now; we'll go pick her up now."

Wayne shook Tom's hand before he left. He could feel the pain and anguish that the drugs could not hide. He wished that he could pull that pain away from Tom. But he knew that Tom had to wither it out.

Wayne and Anita went over to Tom's neighbors and picked up Shari and brought her home with them. She didn't mind going with Wayne and Anita. But she couldn't understand where her daddy was or why her family just disappeared. When she got to Wayne's trailer, she just went into her bedroom and lay in her bed. She dept it up for a couple of days. But, Anita got her to come out to help bathe Wayne Jr. and whenever her father was on the phone.

In the meantime, Wayne was going around trying to get some guidance from the spirited world, but there was no response. It was as though he had to make his decisions by himself. Right now he was going by emotions and knew that he could hurt a lot of people if he'd let his emotions get the better of him. He decided to go ahead full force to get rid of this group that wants to supreme.

February A. 1982.   Wayne went to visit Tom on his lunch break. Tom was recovering from his depression at a very good rate. His hi-light of the day was talking to his daughter, Shari. As soon as the doctor gave him a clean bill of health, and knows that he won't purposely hurt his life or anyone else's he will release him. Then he could return to his daughter.

"Hey bum, you still lurking around here?" Wayne says as soon as he enters Tom's room.

"You got a dollar for a cup of coffee?"

"I don't know; let me see the cup of coffee."

"How you doing today, Wayne?"

"Oh, I guess I'm doing ok. How about yourself?"

"I'm feeling pretty good today. It must be those pills that they give me."

"You better watch it or else you'll become a druggy."

"Have no fear, the doctors are sure that they are non habit forming. How is it going out there?"

"Very slow. I've spent the last couple of days trying to put things together."

"Don't you think that we ought to call in some help?"

"Of a matter of fact, I have given it heavy thought since LA, The group out there pulled a little stunt. I've got to find out how they did it, though."

"What was........."

A nurse came in and Tom stopped in the middle of his sentence.

"It's time for your pills, Mr. Brinkle."

"See not only do they give me pills that make me feel good, but they send in a beautiful girl to boot."

"Maybe I should check into this hospital." Wayne said looking at the nurse. Then something clicked something from the depths of his mind. It seemed so far away and so long ago, but it was there and it was frightening.

"Now Mr. Brinkle I want to see you take these pills before I leave."

The nurse said giving Tom a small paper cup with pills in it.

Wayne then looked at Tom, and tried to make his mind equal with Tom's.

"Tom!"

Wayne yelled in his mind. Tom looked up at Wayne, "Look down, pretend to take them pills; I'll tell you about it later."

Tom put the pills under his tongue, and drank some water.

"That's better Mr. Brinkle, I'm sure that you will be feeling better pretty soon."

"Oh nurse, is it possible that you could send Tom's doctor here? I would like to check with them about getting Tom released."

"I'll see if I could find him."

Then the nurse left the room. As soon as the nurse left the room, Tom spit the pills out into his hand.

92

"What's the problem, Wayne?"

"The problem is that she belongs to that group."

"What! How do you know?"

"I'm not sure, but there is definitely something there."

"What do you want me to do with these pills?"

"Just, hold on to them until the doctor cones in. I want him to have a look at them."

After another five minutes the doctor walked into the room.

"I was told that you wanted to see me."

"Yes doctor, could you tell me what these pills look like?"

"I don't know I'm not a pharmacist, why, where did you get these?"

"A nurse brought them in."

"Well. I'm sure if a nurse brought them in that there's nothing wrong with them."

"Could you at -least find out what you prescribed for him, and if these pills were that drug?"

"I guess I could if it will stop your insistence." The doctor picked up the clip board and turned a couple of pages.

"This isn't at all what was prescribed to him!"

"How about sending it down to the pharmacy and see if they could find out what it is?"

"I'll do that."

And the doctor left the room with the pills. Twenty minutes later the doctor came back into the room.

"Do you remember who gave you these pills?"

"Why, what's the matter with them?" Wayne asked.

"There must have been a mix up somewhere. These are homemade pills; the only thing that these pills will do is kill. That is why I need to know who the nurse was that brought these pills in to you."

"She was just a young beautiful nurse that brought the pills in here on occasion."

Tom said, Wayne was being silent now. His mind was concentrating on the nurse's face. He was sending out until her face became clear, he located her. Now he was looking inside her head, he could see her brain pulsating. Now he concentrated on heat, some cells start to separate rapidly then dissipate. His anger was under control and focused. Her pupils dilated then contract to pin point. Then all of a sudden she couldn't hold her mind anymore. She turned to the nurse standing next to her and said in a childish voice that she pee'd her pants.

Monday, March 3. 1982. Tom was released from the hospital and had been staying with Wayne for a couple of weeks. He didn't want to stay in his house. The memories of that day were too painful for him.

Tom was back to work, but he's sitting behind a desk. They made him an assistant to the editor temporarily. He is fully planning to return to real work.

Wayne had been driving around looking for a place for Tom. The houses were there but nobody was buying now a days. So, Tom was having a lot of trouble selling his house. Wayne brought up the subject that Tom should buy a used trailer and move in the same trailer park as him. So, Tom started checking into trailers.

Wayne decided to take a walk around Public Square for his break today. He wondered why the pigeons stayed around for the winter. He thought that they should have flown south also. The day was cloudy, the ground was wet from a drizzle that threatened to turn into snow. Wayne was beginning to get lost in his thoughts when he felt a twinge. He looked behind him and just saw a middle aged guy that was walking in the opposite direction. It looked as though this guy just passed Wayne.

Wayne has been dealing with the supernatural all of his life, and everyday he learns or progresses in some way. Now that he has to open himself up on all forces around him, he has been able to receive a lot better. When that guy walked by, Wayne's emotions were stirred. At first he didn't know what to make of it; he just stood there in the middle of the square. Then he decided to follow up on his curiosity. He followed the guy through an alley way behind the Leo Mattis book store. He was heading for a parking lot at the other end of the alley. Then the dark feeling of evil came over him.

He knew that this guy was a member of the group. Wayne tried to read this guy's mind to find out information about the group, but the guy looked back at Wayne then started running. So, Wayne had to apply intense concentration heat to the guy's brain. The guy went limp and fell paralyzed. Wayne walked away leaving him mumbling uncertain words.

Before Wayne got off work, he called home and told Anita not to cook dinner. He wanted to take her out to eat. Wayne felt as though he and Anita were beginning to drift apart, and that they needed to get out alone.

Wayne pulled up in the driveway at six o'clock, he noticed that

Tom was already home.

"Hi honey." Wayne said as soon as he entered his trailer. "Are you ready?"

"Yes, Tom said that he'd watch Wayne Jr."

"Are you sure that you're not out of practice, Tom?"

"It's like riding a bicycle, you never forget. You're just rusty," "Okay, well I'm going to wash up then change my clothes."

"Do you need any help?" Anita asked.

"I'm sure that I can do it myself. But, if I whistle come running." It only took Wayne ten minutes to get ready. They drove into Wilkes-Barre for dinner. Wayne decided to go to Aldino's Manor near the Wyoming Valley mall, He thought that he'd go all out on expenses. When they got there, Anita ordered filetmingon and Wayne ordered a Chicken Cordonblu.

"Wayne, I'm glad that we're finally spending some time alone."

"So am I. We haven't really done anything like this in a long time."

"Wayne, I usually don't ask you for anything about what is happening with you, or what's going on with those people, but I am so much in the dark feel that I'm not even a part of your life."

Wayne listened to what Anita just said. He could tell what she was going to say by the first couple of words of her sentence. He could tell that she felt left out, but didn't know exactly how much she was affected by it.

"Okay Anita, I didn't mean to alienate you. What is it that you want to know?"

"First what is it that you are doing now?"

"In a way I'm trying to find all about Jean's and Tommy's death. I am sorting out and trying to find all the members of that group and decrease the total number by leaving them a vegetable. Perhaps if I get enough of them then they will split up and anyone else will be afraid to join.

"How are you going to find them?"

"I have something like an antenna, I am receiving them. At first I wasn't able to receive anything, but it finally came through for me."

"Do you think that it is right to take revenge on them. Isn't it bringing you down to their level?"

"I suppose it is, but it hurt me when I found out how they got me out of town, then did that to Tom's family. They have to pay Anita."

Anita looked at him and could see the pain in his eyes. She could see that even if he doesn't say anything, that he blames himself.

"Is it going to be like this forever? I mean the killings going back and forth."

"Honey, I don't know. I wish that it would end. But, I was put here for some reason. I think if I weren't here that the evil would rein over the world. The group is very big, and I'm fighting the battle by myself. There are many times that I want to give up, but I know that I can't. These people hurt people and torture them, they have to be stopped one way or another.

"Have you ever tried to see what is in the future for me?" Wayne looked at her. Then the waitress brought their food and placed it in front of them. Wayne waited until the waitress left, but he still thought about the question. He didn't want to look into her future. He knew if he looked at her life line on her left palm that it would be short, and her life would show tragedy. But, her right line would show the changes in her life. He loves her too much to even look.

"Anita, my love, for you I could stand anything, except to know what is going to happen to you before it happens. It would kill me to know that something was going to happen, and not being able to do anything." Wayne thought back to the day that Phyllis died. He was wondering if Donnavin really had anything to do with it. Wayne was thinking a lot about Phyllis lately.

"I love you too much to ask you to look into my future, let's eat."

Donnavin had decided once again to just lay back and gain strength through numbers. He knows that Wayne is on the war path and instructed all his followers to stay far away from him, because he became very dangerous since he became revengeful.

Every night they have their ceremonies in a different place. He dare not use Jeffrey Pulp's apartment. He has not been letting Jeffery use his body as much as he used to because he is finding it increasingly harder to control him.

"I can't get a hold of three more members." Delfina said.

"If they don't want to be faithful, then they're not worthy to bother with.   If those peons can't tell by now that I will prevail, then all of them can just go to hell, there I really torment them.   They're all fools; they've been watching too much T.V. and reading too many books. Their whole concept is warped. All the bullshit that they go through, they really believe it. I'm waiting for one day when a couple of those assholes to do something on their own. That will be the last straw. If I didn't need those assholes, I'd get rid of everyone of them," Donnavin said in an apathetical tone.

"Suppose you didn't need me?" Delfina said looking at Donnavin with sad puppy eyes.

"You are faithful; you would always be useful one way or another."

CHAPTER VII

THE STAR'S ABOVE THAT ARE SILENT,
HAVE A MISSION THAT IS RELENT.
THEY COME AMD GO,
BUT THE AVERAGE MAN WOULD NOT KNOW.
LOOK AROUND YOU, ALL YOU SEE IS FACES,
PERHAPS THEY'RE FROM UNKNOWN PLACES.

Saturday, November 13, 1982, Wayne Homza is having a birthday party for Wayne Jr. He's having it down his mother's house in Wilkes-Barre. He figured that it was centrally located there. Most of his nieces and nephews showed up at the party. Tom Brinkle also showed up with Shari. The children were playing their games, while the grownups just talked.

Until this day. Wayne has been burning out the minds of the occult group. He was trying to obtain knowledge from them all, but it was as if a mental block was placed in their heads. He burned out twenty of the devil worshippers. His revenge took him a long way.

Tom found a trailer and moved into it. He lives just a couple of trailers down from Wayne. They occasionally let him do some road work with Wayne but they didn't give that position back to him yet.

Donnavin once again is waiting for things to calm down.

Wayne's rampage is making his followers uneasy. A few times he noticed that a couple of his followers wanted to take matters in their own hands, but Donnavin knew that it would be disastrous, so he put a stop to it before it could happen. His numbers have been growing despite Wayne's ongoing battle with trying to decrease the numbers. People just like the lust, pain and love making, it's their animalistic nature coming out.

Saturday, May 8, 1983. Wayne, (now twenty six years did) was called in to work a half a day. He's working his way up to being the top reporter. He always seems to be the first on the scene. Wayne and Tom have several awards for top rated reporters. They had job offers for bigger T.V. stations, national and local, but they turned them down.

Anita decided to take a ride down to Wilkes-Barre to see Wayne's mother. She called Wayne and told him where she'd be. Wayne Jr., now two and a half years old, went along happily to visit grandma. There he was treated like royalty; he was spoiled, whereas he wouldn't be at home. That irritates Wayne and he let it be known to his mother, but to no avail. She would say that it is a grandma's prerogative.

Anita arrived at her mother-in-law's at ten thirty in the morning. Already the sun was out, and it was a beautiful Pennsylvania day. Anita put Wayne Jr. down in the parlor to play with the toys that they keep there for him. He was totally satisfied with amusing himself. At eleven forty-five a knock came on the door. Katrina asked Anita to see who it was; she was in the cellar taking the clothes out of the washer. Anita went to the door and opened it,

"Yes."

"Is Mrs. Homza in?" Just then Katrina walked up.

"Yes, I'm Mrs. Homza, could I help you?"

"I'm Mr. Hendricks of the health department. We got a call that your house was infested with rodents. I'm afraid that we're going to have to check it out."   He said showing them his I.D. card.

"What!   Are you crazy? Rodents in this house?"

"You don't have let me in without a court order, Mrs. Homza. I could understand especially if you have anything to hide." He said smugly,

"Well Mr. Hendricks, I certainly don't have anything to hide. Come in and try to find something."

"Someone will have to accompany me on my check."

"I will." Katrina said.

"Fine let's start with the upstairs." Katrina went up the stairs first, then Mr. Hendricks followed. Wayne Jr. crawled into the hallway. He could walk fairly well, but he seems to want to reserve his strength. He watched the man walk up the stairs and then his eyes became a glaze, he didn't notice anything around him. Then all of a sudden, the man lost his balance, it seemed as though he went looking for a step that wasn't there and was thrown back head first.

Wayne got out of work at eleven thirty and ran into some

traffic on the way home, so decided to double back and visit his mother. It took him a while to finally reach her house. Too many people were out enjoying the nice day. As soon as he started walking on her porch he started feeling funny. There was some kind of supernatural powers being used there, but he couldn't detect where it was coming from. He felt that way before, but was never able to put a finger on it. He mostly felt it when he was in a heated argument with Anita.

Wayne rushed to the door and opened it. To his astonishment, he was looking at a man falling head first down the stairs. Automatically he pushed an impulse and caught the man in mid air mentally. Then he stood him up straight. Then he looked down at his son. He was broken out of his self made trance and looking at his father like a kid that just got caught with his hand in a cookie jar. The guy just continued walking up the stairs as though nothing had happened.

Anita standing on the side watching the whole thing, just

now noticed that her husband was standing behind her. She turned to look at him, he was looking at Wayne Jr. who was returning

100

his stare.

"Wayne, what is going on here?"

"Our son decided to cause someone to fall down the stairs." Anita looked at Wayne in a shocked disbelieving manner.

"But he's only a baby!"   Anita replied frantically.

"What is going on here with that guy?"

"That, guy is from the health department, and said that someone had reported rodents in this house. Your mother told him that there weren't any kind of rodents, but he was insistent and wanted to check the house, so your mother let him in to check."

"I guess me and Wayne will have to have a little talk."

Mustn't twitch, Wayne thought to himself remembering the old Bewitch's Samantha Stevens sure did have trouble teaching Tabatha not to practice her witchcraft.

Saturday, May 28, 1983. It has been two weeks since the incident with Wayne Jr. Wayne sat his two year old son down and tried to explain to him about what his powers meant and that they weren't meant for evil purposes, or else he would have to punish him. Wayne knew that his son was too young to understand fully. He just figured that he would wait till he was older to explain it more clearly.

Donavan's a patient man waited this whole time in silence. He kept his group as quiet as he was. But the group was now too large to keep too quiet. Donnavin couldn't keep constant control over all his people. As a result there were a few that chose to oppose his silent ways. They thought that they should be heard. So, they started recruiting others in their group, they were very careful, to do it without Donavan's knowledge. They knew that he was able to find out things without asking.

Doug and. Greg were the first two to oppose. Then Doug talked to Brian at Doug's house and convinced him that in order for the group to flourish that they would have to get rid of their enemy once and for all. Greg invited Laura over to his parent's house and convinced her to go with him on this plan.

Their plan was simple. All they had to do was wait for Wayne to go to work and when his wife was alone they then could kill her and the child. It was simple; they didn't know why Donnavin didn't think of that himself. But, he has a lot of complicated things on his mind, so his mind wasn't geared for the simple things, so they thought.

Monday, May 30, 1983. For some unknown reason Donnavin felt very uneasy today. He has mentally and physically searched for the reason that he feels this way, but still can't find it. His thought then went to Wayne Homza.

"Perhaps, he knows that I'm here, maybe he's planning a massive attack on this group. I wonder if he doesn't know that I'm here, and if doesn't know the location of the houses." Donnavin thought to himself.

Meanwhile Wayne was driving to work with a same kind of feeling. He told his wife that he was only going to be at work for as long as he had to. He did not want her to be alone today. He was going to call in but Anita told him not to. She didn't want him to miss work because of her. Greg and Brian were sitting in Greg's '69 Buick Skylark. They were on the roof that was the top of a trailer in the park. They just sat there watching Wayne leave. Doug and Laura are supposed to drive up a little later and get inside the trailer.

After Wayne left they just sat back watching to see if Wayne comes back. At 9:30 a.m. they knew that Wayne wasn't coming back. They knew that in a half an hour Doug and Laura will be coming.

9:45; Anita laid down right after Wayne left, and slept till now. She woke up abruptly in a cold sweat. She looked over at the clock, and then got out of bed to look in on Wayne Jr. and found him playing.

"Do you want to eat breakfast, Wayne?"

"Yeah!" Wayne Jr. says after he looks up at her.

"Well, come on."

"Okay."

Anita walked into the kitchen and poured "Captain Crunch" into a bowl for Wayne Jr. Then went to the refrigerator and found a memo note on the door "Out of milk."

"Oh. I'm sorry Wayne; Mommy forgot that we're out of milk. Do you want to go for a ride to the store to pick some up?"

"Okay, Mommy, I dressed."

Anita went into the bedroom and got dressed. She then picked up the 9 mm colt semi automatic pistol, looked down at it, then put the clip in it and put it in her purse. She remembered back when Wayne gave it to her. She really didn't want it, but now she has grown accustomed to it. Wayne took her to the firing range that was in Wilkes-Barre and showed her how to use it. He taught her the breathing techniques, sturdy hold, and sight picture and sight alignment. She didn't realize that there was such a science involved in shooting a gun. After a couple of practices she became pretty proficient with the gun.

At 9:58 A. M. Anita and her son left the trailer park. They passed a green 1975 Camaro on the road heading towards town. Anita didn't take notice to the car.

Laura was driving the green Camero and was thinking about her open speech to Anita when her walki talk! crackled to life.

"Red leader to blue leader, over."

"This is blue leader go ahead red leader, over."

"Turn around, you just passed the subject, over."

"Roger that, making a one eighty at this time follow them closely, over."

"Follow at this time, over and standing by." The two cars followed Anita until they came to the fork in the road. Anita went left, Laura went right and Greg stayed behind Anita. Laura knew that she would head Anita off where the two roads rejoined all she had to do was go a little bit faster.

"Blue leader to red leader, over."

"This is red leader, go ahead blue leader, over."

"You stay behind the subject; I will head her off at the end. I'll let you know when I'm in position, over."

"Copy that, over."

Anita was not aware of the Skylark following her. Her mind was on Wayne Jr. He hasn't done anything else, but what's going to happen next time he does something. Will his father be there then to reverse the action? She looks down at him: "How can such an innocent looking child have the possibility to be so destructive?" Anita thought to herself.

"Red leader this is blue leader, in position, over."

"Blue leader this is red leader, I'm moving up at this time, over."

Wayne was feeling more and more uneasy as the morning went on. He just couldn't stand the discomposure that had come over him this day. He looked down at his watch: 9:30 A.M. He thought about calling Anita, but she'd think that he was worrying too much so he decided against it. Instead he pulled over into a gas station and picked up the phone to call Tom.

"This is Tom Brinkle, can I help you?"

"Yeah Tom, this is Wayne, can you do me a favor?"

"Sure, what is it Wayne?"

"I need someone to take my place for the rest of the day. Something is going to happen, I just know it. I've got to get home and stay there."

"Sure, no problem, I'll just tell them that you got sick and had to go home."

"Thanks allot; I'm going to head home now."

Wayne gets back on to baby road. He thinks back to the day that he returned to his normal self. That reminds him that even though the group has been stagnant for a year or so, that they might be the ones responsible for his discomforting feeling. To avoid worrying, Wayne started thinking of other things. He started thinking about the old stories related to baby road. And the reason they nick named it baby road.

"I could imagine all the teenagers that popped their cherries parking on the sides of this road. Throughout the decades, there must have been a lot of women getting pregnant" Wayne thought to himself.

"I wonder if that story about that guy getting killed is true. A couple was parked on the side of the road making out, when it started getting late and it was time for them to leave. He went to start his car, and it wouldn't start for some reason. So, the guy told the girl that he was going to go and find a house so that he could call for someone to pick them up. He told her to lock all the doors and to wait till he got back. So he left and she locked all the car doors. As the time went on she got tired and climbed into the back seat and fell asleep. She woke up in the middle of the night to a ping ping noise. It sounded to her like rain drops falling on the roof of the car. She looked around and didn't see her boyfriend anywhere so she went back to sleep. As the sun was rising and shinning into the car it woke her up. Sleepy eyed she looked around for her boyfriend, but he was nowhere to be found. She opened the back door and got out of the car to a rude awakening. The raindrops that she heard were actually blood. She looked up at a tall tree above the car and saw her boyfriend stuck up there hanging. The blood on the car was his, she screamed, and then ran. No one knows how he got up there.

"I wonder if that story is true. You never know what could be roaming these wooded areas. But that story is so old maybe it never happened."

Wayne's mind went to the road and the music playing on the radio. He started taking a curve when his car died. A little bit of fear just went through his body. He let the car roll over to the shoulder of the road and tried to start it, but it was totally dead.

Donnavin as Jeffery Pulp was at work with a similar uneasy feeling as Wayne Homza was experiencing about the same time. He continued to search mentally to find out what the matter was. He continued to look outside the group for some kind of enemy, but couldn't find it. So, he decided to look inside the group for some kind of imposter, when he found out what Doug and Greg had planned. He looked down at his watch; it was 10:00 A.M. too late for him to do anything. He looked around for Wayne Homza, and found him trying to get to his wife in a hurry. He knew that would happen. Those guys ruined allot that he had accomplished the last year. For one split second Wayne's mental eyes locked with Donnavin1s, then Donnavin broke away.

Anita just passed over the bridge and started up hill, she was thinking how beautiful the day looked. Crossing over the bridge she slowed down to hear the brook travel the rocks, then she reached the top of the hill, she noticed a green car blocking the road. The first thing she thought of was the occult, then fear gripped her and she slammed on her brakes. Then she put it in reverse, and started backing up when a Buick was coming up behind her, then set up a road block.

Laura felt like a pro, as she blocked the road. She knew that there wasn't any way for Anita to get around her car. There were trees on both sides of the back road. Laura and Doug deployed from the car and hid in the wooded area, then called in to Greg and Brian that they were ready. All they had to do now was wait. It was only a matter of two minutes when Anita drove up. She stopped at the car blocking the road, and then backed up to the Buick. Doug and Laura sprang into action.

Greg thought that all was lost when he had seen Anita pull off. But he remembered that he had a walki talki, picked it up and used it. Driving down the road he was getting more and more nervous. He was thinking about Wayne Homza and how he either killed or made members mentally retarded. And how Donnavin himself is staying away from him. He thought of what would happen if Wayne drove by while they were shooting his wife and two year old son. For several moments there he was going to back out, but he is now committed and has to see it through. He looked up and saw Anita stop and start backing up towards him. He stepped on the gas pedal and then swung the car around to block the exit. After that he and Brian got out of the car with guns drawn and pointed them at Anita.

Wayne turned the ignition switch of his car, but to no avail. He tried his lights, horn, and radio, but nothing. A weird feeling came over him. He looked up and down the street, but no one was in sight. He got out of his car and lifted the hood up. He took a tire iron and knocked the positive cable to the negative, but got no spark.

"Battery's dead" He thought to himself. He mentally looked around, he didn't see anything. Then all of a sudden it came to him, Anita was in trouble. He could see her in her car and feel the fear that she was feeling. But she was so far away he'd never be able to get to her in time. "Run!" entered his mind, he started jogging. As he was running he came to his senses. He stopped running and mentally tuned in to the situation. He could see a car in front of Anita and she was backing up, but met another car. She then pulled forward. Wayne then looked around and saw the two people waiting to ambush his wife and son. After the car behind Anita stopped, Wayne used his powers and moved that car forward. But all of a sudden the car stopped moving and Wayne's picture went black.

Wayne looked around and noticed that he was in a somewhat of a clearing. He knew his wife was in danger and had to help her, but there was something wrong with his powers, they were gone. He has never felt so helpless before. It was like a bad dream, he was waiting for Anita to wake him out of it anytime now. A loud weird humming noise seemed to come from everywhere. Wayne looked around, but couldn't see anything. The noise got louder and louder till a large object blocked out the sun then hovered over Wayne. Wayne looked up at it then started reaching for his gun. But he stopped and reasoned out that these guys would probably be able to combat such a useless weapon. He also didn't want to aggress against this large machine, since they would be able to kill him with one thought. Then, he wondered if they hadn't neutralized his powers.

Wayne studied the craft with amazement, he no longer feared it. It was like the time he walked around the haunted graveyard. It was a challenge to him. Something was happening up there, he knew it but he didn't know what. There were a lot of voices coming from the craft. As if some mechanical doors were opening and closing. In a flash, Wayne was paralyzed where he stood. There was a greenish blue light with a yellow tinge circling him at his mid-section. It looked to be only about an inch thick, but it was a complete circle around him. It seemed to him to be a little transparent. It seemed to be holding him in place. So he started to feel helpless once again, that made him think of Anita.

Wayne stood there for what seemed to be an endless amount of time. Then the craft finally communicated with him.

"Wayne Homza, we're going to take you with us."

106

"The hell you are!"

"Don't give us any trouble; we need to do some tests on you." "Forget it buddy, there's no way I'm going to leave this planet or my home for that matter, just to be a guinea pig."

"You don't understand, Wayne, you don't have a choice. You are coming with us! "

"Can't you see what's going on in the world? There are forces here that would take over if I was taken away!"

"Wayne Homza, it is not in this world that you belong, you must come with us. If you put up a struggle, we will have to subdue you."

"What do you mean that I don't belong in this world?"

"You are not a full blooded earthling." A voice came out of what seemed to be some kind of loud speaker on the craft. The words hit Wayne hard. He just knew that he was having a nightmare, but no one was waking him up

"You're going to have to explain yourself. I don't understand what you're trying to say to me."

"Decades ago we brought aboard our craft several different women and impregnated them. Once they left the ship they didn't remember ever being on it. We have been monitoring the progress of these half-breed children. A couple died at birth, but most made it to adulthood. There were two that stick out exceptionally well."

"But what does that have to do with me?" Wayne asked hysterically. He didn't want to read into what exactly they were saying.

"Your mother was one of those women on board. And Donavan's mother came aboard a couple of your earth years before."

"No. you're lying to me!"

"Yes Wayne, you have been fighting against your own brother all those years. We have no reason to lie to you, we won't gain anything. We already have you."

Wayne feels a tinge of fear, then it gets stronger, but the fear is not his, it's applied from an outside source. Someone else is very afraid and he is receiving it, but whom?"

"Anita, Anita is in trouble. I totally forgot about her."

Wayne said looking down at the ground. He tried hard to follow that emotion to his wife, but he was still contained by the strange air craft. His own emotions started to come to their peak. His love for his wife and son took his mind off the craft. He started concentrating on the light circling him. He tried to make it circle the opposite way. It then stopped and started going the other way. Then it started going faster and faster until it disappeared. Wayne was then free. He looked up at the craft and noticed that it started teetering.

It was not hovering level anymore. It looked like smoke started to come out of it. Then it just took off, leaving Wayne stand there wondering.

Anita went by the Buick too fast, her car bumped the Buick which made her bounce off of it and into the woods. When she finally stopped her car, she was two feet away from the brook that she slowed down to listen to just moments ago. She just then remembered the gun in her purse; she looked around for it with her hand, and then pulled it out. After that she grabbed Wayne Jr. and carried him out of the car, by then she could see some people running towards her from the road. She stopped by a tree, took aim at the first person that was in the clear, she made sure that she lead him first, then squeezed the trigger. It was a shock and made her jump and Wayne screamed and started crying. She opened her eyes and noticed that the guy was on the ground and not moving, and then a girl ran over to him.

"Greg! Greg!" Laura yelled while she ran over to Greg's body that lay still on the ground. Brian and Doug came over almost immediately afterwards.

"She killed him! That bitch killed him! You bastard! I'll kill you; I swear I'll kill you, bastard!"

"Well Doug, what are we going to do now, she has a gun." Brian asked Doug while looking around in the woods, expecting another shot to ring out in their direction.

"We're going to kill that bitch, that's what we're going to do!" Laura shouted.

"She's right, you know. Our prey is only a woman and she's carrying a kid at that. If we rationalize, we should be able to kill her and her kid. Then, we would lay a trap for her hubby." Doug answered. They looked in the direction of Anita's car, then split up and worked their way towards it by running from tree to tree.

Anita was hiding behind a tree that was close to the one that she used for cover to shoot Greg. She just stayed there watching the other people that were trying to kill her. She was trying very hard to calm Wayne Jr. down so that he would not give out their position. She was hoping that they would just leave so that she could find a way home. But, they didn't and they're coming to get her. She now has to use her gun again to save their lives. She looked down at Wayne Jr., he became unusually quiet. He was just standing there staring.

Anita took aim once more; she aimed at the closest person to her, then squeezed the trigger. She missed, she was breathing too heavily, and she quickly re aimed held her breath. This time Doug dropped to the ground. But, another gunshot was heard from behind her, she quickly whirled around getting close to the ground and putting Wayne Jr. behind her. Laura was aiming her gun at Anita, but Anita fired from the waist and got Laura in the stomach before Laura could fire again. Laura bent over in pain, and as she did her gun dropped to the ground. Anita just looked at her, then she remembered that there was one more guy left. She quickly turned around trying to move Wayne Jr. in a safe spot. Through the tears of fear she could see a guy running away from her.

After the craft left, Wayne immediately tuned in to what was happening to his family. He saw Anita in a wooded area and she had her gun in her hands, but there was a girl sneaking up behind her and she didn't know it. The girl aimed at Anita's head, which was when Wayne interrupted and made the girl miss. Then Anita turned around and shot the girl. Wayne then scanned the rest of the area for anyone else, and found a guy running away from the area. Wayne let him run to the car. Brian started it up, put it in gear, and then drove off. Wayne then made Brian push the accelerator to the floor and he froze the steering wheel. The car went right into a tree with a loud explosion.

Anita thought about shooting Brian in the back, but chose against it. She watched him run into his car before she did anything. But when his car rammed into a tree, she knew that, Wayne's thoughts were with her and that she didn't have anything else to worry about. Behind her Laura had fallen to the ground clutching her stomach. Her death was that of a painful one.

Wayne made a passer-by go the same way that the accident was. The passerby made a phone call to the police, and then she fled so as to not get involved. After that Wayne walked back to his car, got inside it, placed the key in the ignition, then turned it. As Wayne suspected, the car started. He headed towards home at a fast rate.

Anita takes Wayne Jr. to the road and sits down on the grass. She knows that somehow Wayne will send her some help, and all she has to do is wait. Within twenty minutes a patrol car pulls up. The two patrolmen had already stopped by the smoldering wreckage, then sees Anita just sitting on the grass. They walked up to her, she stood up and told them what had happened. She then showed them where the bodies were. After the ambulance arrived and a few more patrol cars, the first two patrolmen took Anita and Wayne Jr. to the hospital.

Donnavin watched the whole thing through his mind's eye.

After he looked with Wayne's mind, he discontinued watching Wayne. He continued to watch Anita and knew that something was wrong when Wayne wasn't helping her. But, he did see Wayne's help near the end of the battle. He knows now that Wayne will come at him with all the force that he could muster up.

Donnavin looks back at his past, how wonderful it was with a little or no oppositions. Then Wayne came along and started putting real blocks in front of his plans. To make things worse, the body that he was born with was destroyed by Wayne. Donnavin knows that his group would not withstand another attack by Wayne, when Wayne comes he's going to use all his energies to wipe the group out. Wayne is too protective of his family to let this go by. Donnavin will have to call his other memberships in order to got reinforcements. And he's going to have to screen his followers a lot from now on in order to keep them in line.

11:30A.M. It was all over with now, and Donnavin still pondered what just took place. He had to take the rest of the day off to coordinate things with his other members in order to get ready for Wayne's wrath. He complains to his boss that he's sick and goes home.

Wayne gets on to I-81 figuring that it will be the fastest route to Shickshinny. His mind was filled with anger because this group just tried once more to take the life of his family, and worry for his wife and child. Hoping that there wasn't any mental damage done to either one of them. His concentration was not on the road; therefore it would take awhile for whatever he saw to register. That's why when he saw a car in a ditch he didn't immediately stop. But, a mile down the road the image of the car and somebody trapped in it came to his mind.

Wayne knew that his wife was alright, so he pulled off the road and backed up to the other car. When he reached there, he noticed that steam was forcing its way out from under the hood. He quickly put his car in park, got out, and ran over to the other car. The first thing he noticed was a body slumped over in the driver's seat. He walked over to the door and opened it. He looked at the body, just a teenage girl. He scanned the aura to where the damages were and noticed that that the head was the only place of injury. Wayne carefully slid the girl out of the car and on to the ground. He

110

noticed that she was bleeding profusely from the head, so he started concentrating to heal her.

As Wayne was concentrating to heal the girl, he didn't notice anything going on around him. His mind was totally on the girl's wound. Suddenly Wayne felt something over his face, then he was sound asleep. "Hey men, this chloroform stuff really works."

"Stop yelling and help me get him into the car."

"Why don't we just waste him right here?"

"Because Doug wants us to take him back to the abandon house. Besides, I'd like to have some fun with him myself."

"What about Rosalee?"

"We're going to have to leave her here for someone else to find. She knew what she was doing from the start. Now let's hurry up and get out of here, we're already late for meeting Doug."

The two guys picked Wayne up and put him in their car. Then, one got into Wayne's car and drove off.

In the Heights section of Wilkes-Barre where the group used

to meet, a couple of group members await the arrival of Wayne Homza, none of which has any idea as to what had happened to Doug and the other three. They think that Doug is on his way back from a victorious killing. Wayne's car drives up, then gets pulled around the back. Another car pulls up, a couple people from the membership go out to help drag Wayne into the house, kicking him on the way, until he started Jerking on them. Someone ran back to the car and brought back with him some chloroform and applied it to Wayne once again, which made him settle down.

They took him down the cellar, but stopped kicking him, figuring that's what woke him up. There were ropes nailed to the wall in the cellar. Around the one spot of the wall were bottles of chloroform. The members of the group brought Wayne to that spot of the wall and tied his hands and feet to it, then just left him dangling. After that they unscrewed the bottles of chloroform, then departed.

"Has anybody seen or heard from Doug?" Alex, one of the guys that picked up Wayne from the highway, asked.

"No, they should have finished the job by now." Andrea an old member of the group answered.

"I hope that nothing has gone wrong." Alex stated.

"Suppose something has gone wrong, what do we do with him?" Andrea asks.

"Well, if we leave him hang there, he will die of asphyxiation, but we're not going to let him get off that easy. We're going to make him pay for what he did to our group. Just as long as he doesn't wake up, we have nothing to worry about.

Tuesday, May 31, 1983. Wayne Homza was now near death. His body was healthy and strong, but could not deal with this. Alex had a couple of the members go down to bring Wayne out into the fresh air. They will revive him but only so far.

As far as Wayne is concerned, he is sleeping. His conscious mind knows not of what is happening to him. They caught him off guard and they are keeping him that way. But once his physical body is being threatened with death, Wayne himself starts to become aware as to what is happening. But before he could do anything his body is brought into fresh, air, where he is not threatened anymore with death.

Monday May 30, 1983. Tom Brinkle was driving around in his car when he heard the dispatcher of the state police dispatch a patrol car to an accident near Wayne's house. Tom immediately reported to the situation, but by the time that he got there it was all over and the coroner was removing the bodies out. Tom shows his press card and goes inside the roped off area, and walks up to the guy investigating the incident.

"Hal! What happened here?" Tom asks as he approaches the guy.

"Oh hi Tom, it's been a long time since I've seen you, how've you been?"

"I've been ok. I was in a slump for a while there after my wife and boy died,"

"Yeah, I was sorry to hear about that. I was going to go the funeral but I was stuck on a case and couldn't get away."

"That's okay thanks for the card."

"It was the least I could do."

"Now, what happened here?"

"You wouldn't believe it in this day and age. A couple of kids tried to run a woman and her baby off the road. And then after that they started shooting at her!"

"Who was she?" Tom asked, but he knew what the answer was going to be. Hal took out a notebook from his top shirt pocket, opened it to a page,

"Anita Homza and her son Wayne. Hey, you know these people, don't you?"

"Yeah, the whole family is very close to me. Were any of them hurt?"

"No, that little lady is a very good shot, and resourceful."

"Thank God, where are they now?"

"An ambulance took them to the hospital just to make sure that they're alright. Do you know where her husband is? We called your office and they said that he had already gone home."

"No. I don't know where he is; I thought that he would already be here. There's my camera men I better go see to them."

Tom stayed in that area until he saw the state police car bring Anita back. Then, he followed her to her trailer. After knocking on the door he stepped inside.

"Tom! Where's Wayne?" Anita asks as soon as she sees Tom.

"I don't know Anita. He should have been here by now; I took his place several hours ago so that he could come home."

"Well then, where is he?"

"I'm going to call a friend of mine at the police station, he'll put a missing persons out, even though it hasn't been twenty four hours."

Donnavin arrived at home and Delfina was there to greet him.

"What's wrong? I've sensed your vibes all morning!"

"Those insolent fools, how dare they cross me! I've got to call the other houses, I have to get as much people as possible. Wayne will be on a warpath."

"You mean our people tried to kill him?"

"No worse, they tried to kill his wife and kid."

"He certainly wouldn't stand still for that."

"The thing is that he did. He didn't help her until it was almost all over with."

"Why would he wait that long to save his wife? That's not like him at all."

"I know, something must have happened, and I can't even find out what."

Donnavin went ahead and made those calls. Then he went into his study so that he could meditate on formulating a plan.

Alex sat by his portable radio most of the day until he heard the broadcast about Anita Homza being attacked and killing her attackers.

That is when he knew that Doug was not going to show up at the house. Fear started entering his body. He started thinking about what Wayne would do if somehow he would come out of it and get loose. For a few moments there, he wasn't sure what to do next. He knew that he and the others at that house couldn't go near Donnavin until it was over, otherwise he would find out what they had done. And even though they do have Wayne Homza subdued, they still defied Donnavin. They will have to wait till Wayne is dead and bring Donnavin his body

Alex started to calm down and get rid of his fears. He knew that he wanted to have some fun with Wayne before he killed him. So, he decided to leave him down the cellar overnight, and then if Wayne is still alive, he'll have his fun in the morning.

After Donnavin made his mental plans, he went in the bedroom and had afternoon sex with Delfina. He found that with, this younger body, he was able to become more physical than with the old one that he lost during the battle. As his mind pondered on different situations that has arisen and may arise, he couldn't help but think that something else was going to happen. That the attack with Wayne's wife wasn't the only thing that his disobedient followers had planned. But he can't find anything else that is going on. Either some of his members found a way to keep things from him or there isn't anything going on.

Tuesday, May 31. 1983. Anita lay awake in bed all night wondering what had happened to her husband. When she opened the door yesterday and only saw Tom Brinkle and not Wayne, her heart fell. She knew that if everything was alright, Wayne would have come straight home. She got out of bed at 7:00 A.M. went into the bathroom to wash the tears off her face, then she went into the kitchen where she found Tom perking coffee, Tom's little girl Shari and Wayne Jr. were both still asleep.

"Good morning Anita, did you get much sleep last night?"

"Not a wink. I was waiting for Wayne to walk in with a smirk on his face and say that his car broke down or something."

"I know what you mean, I lay awake all night just waiting for him to show up."

"I just can't understand what happened to him, or why that group all of a sudden made an attack on us."

"Well, don't worry too much, I've seen Wayne in action against the leader of the group, and he was the toughest one. Now that he's gone there's no one that could ever come close to him."

"Then where is he? Don't forget that he was weakened from that fight. He never fully recovered from it either."

"Where he was weakened in some areas, he has strengthened in others. He can still fend off any attack. I just don't want to see you get all worked up over this. I know that Wayne doesn't want to see you get sick over him missing."

"I can't help it he's   ."

"Mommy, I seen daddy last night." Wayne Jr. interrupted as he walked into the living room rubbing his eyes.

Anita turned around startled. For a moment she was speechless. Different things raced through her mind. First she thought that he made it up, but then thought that Wayne Jr. inherited some of his father's powers.

"What do you mean, honey?" Anita asked while picking Wayne Jr. up."

"Daddy came into my room, he didn't say anything, and he just stood like he always does, then he went away."

"Are you sure it was daddy?"

"Yes mommy,   what's wrong,   Where's daddy?"

"I wish I knew honey, but daddy didn't come home last night. I think his car broke down or something."

"Daddy would know how to fix it."

"Maybe, we'll find out when he gets home."

The members threw Wayne to the ground. They stared at his limp body then spit on him.

"This guy isn't so tough, why was everybody afraid of him?" One member said to the other.

"I don't know, they say he defeated Donnavin, but you know how rumors go."

"Get the rope and tie his hands behind his back." Alex said as he walked out the door.

"But, you don't have to worry about him, he's almost dead, he isn't going to do anything!"

"Just do as I say!"

The member reluctantly went to get the rope. He came back and rolled Wayne onto his stomach, then tied his hands behind him. He looked at the sky while tying Wayne; He noticed how blue the sky looked. A lazy white cloud drifted by. it was turning out to be a nice day. He looked down at Wayne as he pulled the rope tighter as to cut off the circulation, Wayne's hands flicked, his fingers curled into fist. The member then rolled Wayne on his back.

"What are we going to do to him now Alex, shoot him?"

"No, that would be too quick, I want him to feel pain and agony. Get a bucket of cold water." Alex then went into the back yard and picked up a rubber water hose.

"What do you want me to do with this water, Al?"

"Throw it on him; make sure you get it all over his body." The member threw the water all over Wayne, as a matter of fact he even went and got some more water for Wayne, After Wayne was totally wet, Alex stood over him with the hose, and started whipping Wayne with it, Alex's eyes became glassy, and he only stared as he continued to whip Wayne with no mercy.

The two members watched Alex in awe. When Alex first started beating Wayne he was doing it with style. But now he's just beating and Wayne is just lying there. Then things started to happen, the hall door would open and close with no one there, a gusty wind just picked up. The two members started to get worried, so they started to call Alex's name, but he didn't answer. They started nudging his shoulder, but still no response. So they finally grabbed him and pulled him away from Wayne. Alex looked up at them with a frightening look on his face.

"Throw him back down the cellar!" Alex said and went back inside the house. The members drug Wayne to the top of the stairs, and then let him roll down the steps. His body making heavy thudding noises as he bounced from step to step. Then the door was slammed shut as Wayne's body rests at the bottom of the stairs. A trickle of blood forming at his nose and drying on to the wet damp floor.

"When are we going to kill him." One of the members asked Alex.

"Just as soon as I get my sword ready." Alex went to get a sword from the second floor bedroom. Then he and the other two sat around it and chanted.

Wayne's body was motionless, but his spirit was restless. It had to be free from the body, because the body could hardly sustain life anymore. Wayne's spirit is becoming more and more aware of what is going on in the house, so he quickly reacts.

Alex heads down stairs from the second floor. His sword is in his hand ready to decapitate Wayne's head. When he reaches the bottom floor he heads towards the basement door, he hears the sound of water pouring, but he ignores it. When he reaches the basement door, he stands back holding the sword with two hands, and lets one of the members open the door."

"Hey Alex, the door's stuck!"

"What! Let me try it." The other member replies.

"He's right, I can't get this damn door open.

"Well, both of you try it, it shouldn't be that hard for two people,"

"We just can't get it open Alex, maybe he's at the other end holding it closed."

"Don't be stupid, there's no way that he could ever walk more or less hold a door closed from two people." Alex said while putting the sword down to try the door.

"This one doesn't open either!" A member says frantically, while trying to open the kitchen door. Alex looks back at him, picks up the sword, and then starts to hack away at the basement door. The wood started to chip away, and then the sword breaks in half with a loud shattering noise. The vibrations were so hard that it made Alex drop the sword.

After Alex dropped the sword, the other member ran to the front door and tried to open it to no avail. Then he went around to each and every window in the house and tried to open them, but they wouldn't budge. He then picked up a chair and threw it at the window repeatedly but the only thing that broke was the chair. When he turned around Alex was standing there watching him.

"What is going on Alex? How can this be?"

"I don't know, but I can't be defeated. We'll get together and chant for strength to overcome this slight obstacle."

Wayne's battered body couldn't move due to the thickness of the chloroform in the air. The only way out of it was to cleanse the air, so he created a larger hole in the main water line, thus spraying water everywhere on the cement floor. Within moments the floor was covered with water. The cool water soothed Wayne's aching body, and disrupted the chloroform that was in the air.

By the time Wayne was slowly coming out of it, he was already floating face down in three feet of water. The water loosened the ropes binding his hands behind him. It didn't take much effort for him to free his hands. He then created a block of wood to float over to him. As soon as it got close enough, he put it underneath his shoulders, and floated with his head above water.

7:00 P.M. The water was now ceiling level. Wayne was very weak but awake. He paddled his feet (as best as he can) over to the cellar window and pushed it open. He then made himself roll out of the window, quickly closing it behind him. He was so weak; that he couldn't even crawl he just laid there to gather strength.

At seven o'clock it was starting to get dark, so Alex got up to turn the lights on, but he found out that they wouldn't come on. He went through the hallway trying all the lights, but they wouldn't come on either. So he went down stairs to try those lights, but when he walked across the floor he heard the splish splash sound of water beneath his feet. He quickly went into the kitchen to check the water faucets and found them to be alright. Then he looked over at the cellar door, and found it ajar. Fear entered his body.

"Dan, Len, get down here fast!" Alex screamed as he stood at the door. The two of thorn bolted down the stairs.

"What's the matter, Al? Where'd this water come from?" Dan said trudging through the water.

"Down there it's from down there."

"What about Wayne?" Dan asked.

"I hope the fucker drowned," Alex shouted, "What are we going to do now? Lenny asked,

"Someone has to go down there and try to stop the water," Alex stated.

"I'll go down, I'm a pretty fair swimmer," Lenny replied. He opened the cellar door further, the water on the on the steps somewhat hindering his efforts. He walked down the steps part way then dove into the water, within seconds he disappeared, 8:00 P.M. The house is dark now, and tie water in the kitchen is knee deep. Alex and Dan just sat on the kitchen chairs,

"He's not coming up," Dan said grimly.

"Let's go upstairs to drier ground; this water has to seep out somewhere, before morning."

"Suppose Lenny comes up while we're up there. How would he know where to find us?"

"If Lenny came up he would automatically go upstairs."

"Is there any way that you could get some help from someone? Maybe Donnavin."

"Even if I could reach Donnavin. I don't think that he will help us. He tried to tell us how dangerous this guy was."

"But how could he do all this, he was nearly dead."

"Remember this guy defeated Donnavin."

One o'clock in the morning the water is ankle deep on the second floor Alex, as a last resort, started concentrating on Donnavin, He tried to picture Donnavin in his mind but all he could get was the back side of him and he was walking away. Now he knew for sure that Donnavin wasn't going to help him. Fear groped him once more and he tried to break the windows, and kept on screaming for help but no one could hear him, except Dan.

Donnavin was able to see what was happening and could have let the water out of the house. But, he could not let Wayne know that he was on earth. He knew that Wayne was going to retaliate, but he wanted to keep the element of surprise on his side. Besides, it's going to take Wayne awhile to recover from this, so that would give him more time to devise a better plan.

8:00 A.M. Wednesday, June 1, 1983. Wayne (still lying where he crawled out to) awakens, he knows now that both Alex and Dan had breathed their last in the water. The house could no longer hold the water, it started springing leaks, then one of the front bottom windows just gave way. The water was gushing out of the window and onto the street flooding it like it has never been flooded before. Wayne heard the noise of the water expelling from the house, so he tried to get up, but his legs couldn't support him, so he crawled.

Mrs. Pendle was the first to call the police about the water rushing down the hill. She was an elderly woman and lived alone. Most of her senses were going with age, but she could still hear pretty well. She heard the water rushing by, and ran to the window to see what it was. Then she got flashbacks from Agnes, and the flood of '72. She lived in south Wilkes-Barre at that time. She had to be carried out of her house and onto a boat, in order to escape the waters. She moved up to the Heights, because she thought that she'd be free from anymore floods,

When the police received the call, they thought that a main water line busted, so they called the Pennsylvania gas and Water Co. The P. G and W sent a crew over to the area immediately. When they saw the water all over the place, they radioed in to have the main water line for the area turned off.

When the police arrived, they immediately sought to find the origin of the water. Finally after a half an hour of driving around, they noticed a small seepage coming from a house. They got out of their vehicle and walked over to it. The first cop almost stumbled over Wayne on his way. He instantly told his partner to call for an ambulance.

Wednesday. June 1, 1983. Tom Brinkle really didn't want to go to work today. He'd rather stay at Wayne Homza's house in case Anita needed him for anything. But, he knew that Anita could take care of herself and that he would probably be of more assistance on the road looking for Wayne. He knows that Wayne has saved his life a countless number of times. He feels that he owes Wayne such gratitude that could never be repaid. Although Wayne wasn't there to save Tom's wife and child, there is no one else to blame but that group for their death,

8:45 A.M. Tom was driving along North Penna. Ave, when he heard on the police scanner, that there was water flooding the streets in the Heights section of Wilkes-Barre, with an unknown cause. Tom knew that if Wayne could give some kind of signal that this would be it. So, he turned around and headed for the Heights. He drove to the street that Mrs. Pendle lived on and first sighted the water. There were road blocks already set up by the time he got there. After a few detours he finally managed to get near the house where the water came from.

When Tom drove up he noticed a body on a stretcher with an oxygen mask covering the person's face. He started walking towards the stretcher when a policeman stopped him. He showed him his press I.D. and went on. He reached the ambulance just before they put the stretcher in.

"Wait a minute!" Tom shouted as he approached the ambulance. The attendants stopped and looked at him. Tom then took a look at the body.

"Oh my God! is he alright?"

"Do you know this man?" One of the attendants asked.

"Yes, he works for my T.V. station. Is he going to be alright?"

"I really couldn't say for sure, but you better notify his immediate family, he doesn't look too good."

"Okay, what hospital are you taking him to?"

"The General seems to be the easiest to get to."

Tom went to the house next door, identified himself and asked to use the phone. He called Anita and told her that Wayne was alive, but in the General Hospital. He told her that he'd meet her there later that he had to finish covering a story. Then he asked the lady some standard questions, and left. When he got outside; his cameramen had just rolled up in their van. He started issuing orders to them and walked around talking into the microphone. He noticed Dan's body that was slumped over the windowsill, ambulance personnel were just getting him on a stretcher. They walked down the street and seen another body (Lenny) draped over the top of a car. Tom looked closer at him and noticed that there was a hole in his hand. Then Tom looked around and was stunned at the hideous sight before his eyes. Across the street on a telephone pole about seven feet up was a body of a man, (Alex) his side was stuck in one of the spikes that the repairmen use to climb the pole, and he was just hanging by his side with the spike slowly ripping through his flesh.

Anita was doing the morning dishes when the phone rang. She didn't feel much like eating breakfast, but Wayne Jr. and Shari ate all of theirs'. As soon as she heard the phone ring her heart dropped. She ran over to it hesitated, then answered it. After she hung up the phone, she had mixed feelings. She knew that her husband was alive, but she didn't know what shape he was in. She has always feared a relapse of him returning to child like state. She picked up the phone and called Wayne's mother, and explained the situation to her, then dropped the kids off at her house, Wayne's mother in turn called all of Wayne's relatives, including his mother-in-law.

When Anita arrived in the emergency room at the General Hospital, she went straight to the desk to ask about her husband. The nurse at the desk told her that the doctor was in with her husband now, and that they would get back to her. Then she told her to have a seat.

When Wayne entered the hospital his breathing was shallow, his pulse was weak and thready, and his blood pressure was low and weak. The doctor ordered all different kinds of blood tests immediately and had the nurses hook up an electro—cardiogram machine. All of Wayne's vital signs were bad; as soon as the doctor found out Wayne's blood type he ordered a pint of whole blood.

As Anita was waiting in the waiting room, Wayne's relatives were trickling in.

"How is he?" Katrina asked as soon as she saw Anita.

"I don't know, they said that the doctor was with him and that he will tell me as soon as he knows,"

"Do you want to get some coffee or tea it might calm your nerves?" Katrina asked,

"No thank you, I want to be here in case the doctor comes. You could go though."

"How about if I bring you back a cup?"

"Okay, make it hot chocolate"

Wayne started to cough spastically, the doctor ordered shots to relax his muscles, but it was too late. The too familiar Beeeep sound of the EK G was now sounding.

"Get the defibrillator unit!" The doctor shouted and started external cardiac massage.

"One thousand one, one thousand two, one thousand three, one thousand four, one thousand five." The doctor counted aloud, and then the nurse would squeeze a ball which force oxygen onto Wayne's lungs.

Just before Wayne's heart stopped, his spirit bolted from his body. It stayed hovering near ceiling over his body. Then another spirit came into the room and went next to Wayne's. Wayne's first impression was comfort; it was as if he knew this spirit. He couldn't recognize anything about this spirit, there was no shape or form, just a ball of light.

The doctor hooked the defibrillator machine up, put cream on the plates, and then placed the plates on Wayne's chest.

"Clear, Hit it!" The doctor yelled to the technician. Wayne's body jerked furiously.

"Again!" And Wayne's body jerks again. Then the doctor goes back to continually massaging the heart.

1:15 P.M. The doctors now have been trying to revive Wayne for three hours; with no success. The doctor looks up at the clock.

"How long has it been now?" The doctor asked the nurse. The nurse looks up at the clock.

"It has been three hours now, doctor."

"What is his name?"

"Homza, Wayne Homza."

With that information the doctor walks out to the waiting room.

"Mrs. Homza?" Anita and Katrina stand up.

"Come this way." The doctor says pointing through the doors; He walked down into an unoccupied room.

"I'm sorry Anita, Katrina, we lost him."

11:30 A.M. Wayne forces himself out of his body and drifts towards the ceiling. He looks down at the doctors working on his body. The pain that his body was in was too much for him to bear. When he leaves his body, he is more aware of his surroundings. It is a relieved feeling. He knows the intense drama that is going on below him. The nurses and doctors searching through their minds as how to save this man's life.

A new awareness came to Wayne; a feeling that he hasn't felt before. He looks around the room and sees a light coming from the far corner. The light was slowly floating towards him. It was emitting a glow of goodness and warmth. Wayne felt very comfortable with this light as if he knew it all his life.

"You really blundered this one, didn't you Wayne?" The entity says to him.

"I guess I did, they took me by surprise."

"Through all you've been through, you still trust these humans."

"I can't help it, it's my nature, I have to help people, that's one of the reasons that I'm here."

"Are you ready to come with me?"

"No, my mission here is not fulfilled yet!"

"This is most irregular, most people rejoice to follow me, and when they're told to go back, they don't want to."

"I'm not most people, you know that!"

"Yes, I guess I do. Well, are you sure that you want to go back?"

"Yes."

"Okay, I can't force you to come with me. So if you're going to return to your flesh form then you better do so before any denigration begins, to occur"

Wayne looks down at his body, and notices that the doctors are walking out of the room, the nurses are disconnecting all the equipment that is connected to Wayne, (Time while being out of his body had no elements to it.) Just before the nurses disconnected the E. K. G. Wayne entered his body. The pain in his chest was excruciating. Then the straight line on the E. K. G. scope jumped noticeably and then jumped again.

"No wait!" One of the nurses looked at the screen.

"I'll get the doctor!" She replied.

It's one thing for a doctor to lose a patient, but he also has to tell the loved ones. Doctor Brieker really didn't want to tell Wayne's wife and mother, but he knew he had to. The two of them just broke down and cried, the other members of the family that there could see the two of them crying and knew immediately that Wayne had died. The doctor just put his head in his hands and felt the sadness of the people in front of him, until he heard the nurse come screaming his name.

"Doctor Brieker, Doctor Brieker."

"What is it nurse?" The doctor replied grabbing her by her shoulder.

"It's the patient doctor, his heart started again." The doctor turned and looked at her with an expression that the nurse has never seen on his face before. He then bolted for the door to the room that Wayne lay in.

Thursday, June 2. 1983. Wayne had been in the intensive care unit all night under close observation. So when his eyes blinked open, a nurse was on hand to call the doctor. Doctor Brieker was just coming on, so he walked briskly to check on Wayne.

"Good morning Wayne, and how are you feeling today?" The doctor asked as he read the chart that was hanging on the bottom of the bed.

"A lot better than yesterday," Wayne said in a scratchy voice.

The doctor walked up to Wayne, then lifted his eyelids and shone a penlight

into his eyes.

"You know you gave us quite a scare yesterday,"

"Yeah, well you know that you kind over reacted too." The doctor gave him an inquisitive look.

"How long are you going to hold me in here doc?"

"By the looks of your chart, a couple of weeks."

"If my health improves will you let me out of here today?"

"I don't think that you'd get better that quick."

"But if I do, will you let me out this afternoon?"

"I could safely say, that if you get that much better by this afternoon, I will let you out."

"Okay. I'm going to hold you to that, doc."

CHAPTER VIII

A STATE OF PHANTASMAGORIA,
WILL MAKE YOU THINK YOU'RE IN A BURIAL.
YOU WILL FIGHT A MYTHICAL OGRE,
THAT WILL COME BACK OVER AND OVER.
YOU WILL BE ABLE TO FLY LIKE SUPERMAN,
AND RETURN UPON YOUR COMMAND.
RUN FROM A BEAST WITH LEGS OF LEAD,
ONLY TO AWAKE IN BED.
BE ABLE TO FLOAT AROUND,
AND FIND THAT YOU ARE NOT BOUND.
AT TIMES YOU WILL DISCOVER,
THAT YOU ARE A GREAT LOVER.
VISIT PLACES NEVER BEEN BEFORE,
WITHOUT EVEN GOING NEXT DOOR.
THAT IS THIS GREAT MYSTICAL BEAM?
LOOK TO YOUSELF, IT'S ONLY A DREAM.

The doctor left and Wayne closed his eyes. Images drifted in and out, like a movie, showed frame by frame. Then Wayne drifted off to a sound restful sleep. Dreams entered and left, but on came and stayed until he woke up.

It is dark, perhaps night time. Wayne is unaware of his surroundings. He starts walking and looks up; he could barely see the moon through a thick haze. He sees that he is on a street, but there aren't any people around him. He continues to walk down the street, and hears fainted cries in the distance. All of a sudden something swoops down from the sky and knocks him down to the ground. He hits the ground hard and is unable to move, he could hear a flapping sword coming nearer and nearer. He finally rolls underneath a porch, and then hears something slithering towards him. He rolls back out again and starts running. He sees an alley and turns down it. Then he steps dead in his tracks and hears a spine chilling snarl in the distance ahead of him. His eyes open wide with fear, he tries to scream but can't. Wayne is looking down at a bull dog pulling itself towards him, with no hind quarters. Its guts are being dragged behind it. Now it makes ready for the attack. Wayne starts backing up and the dog matches him step for step. Wayne looks back and sees that he's on a back road and starts to run again. He looks to the left and sees a cave; he passes it off then runs on to the shoulder of the road and stops. He hears feet running down the road, so he walks backwards towards the cave. All of a sudden everything gets black, he feels as though he's in the cave, then a hand rests on his shoulder, his stomach quivers as adrenalin starts flowing, he shoots out of the cave like a dart.

Wayne finds himself at a construction site on a dirt mound. Construction equipment is all around him. He looks up at the yellow back hoe that stands in front of him quiet. Images of it digging holes in the daytime runs through his mind. He turns away from it to see where he's at, and hears a squeaking sound. He turns back and sees that the back hoe is still, but there was something different about it. He walks closer to it to get a better look. He looks at it, and then notices the bucket, it was upturned to give the machine support, but now it's in the scoop position. Wayne looks again at the seat and sees that no one is there, so he says to himself that he must have imagined the whole thing, and starts walking away.

He looks at the tractor and it seemed to move close to him, then the dump truck seemed to be closing in on yet another side. He looks back at the back hoe and the bucket is facing him now where it was facing away from him before. Wayne hears a diesel engine start up; he looks towards the sound and sees the pay loader slowly moving towards him. Then, the other machines start their engines, and turn their lights on Wayne. Wayne looks around at the machines; the lights look like eyes, and the front screens look like mouths. He could almost see them smiling even leering at him.

The back hoe takes a swipe at him with that long arm it has.

Wayne dodges it by shoulder rolling under the dump truck. The dump truck then moves back and forth trying to run Wayne over. It then just takes off to get out of the way of the other machines and when it does the back hoe was there to greet Wayne. It dropped the bucket right at Wayne. But he seen it in time and rolled away from it. The pay loader was at the other end of his roll, and scooped him up, to drop him in the dump truck. The dump truck in turn dropped him back on the ground where the tractor went charging towards him.

Wayne got up and ran but the back hoe swung its big arm and knocked Wayne down once again. Wayne noticed that the tractor was still charging at him with full speed. Wayne quickly rolled under the dump truck and then rolled out the other side, then got up. After that he heard a loud crash and saw the dump truck get rocked onto its side, and lay with the tires spinning. On the other side of it was the tractor. The tractor backs up and lowers its shovel slightly.

Meanwhile the pay loader filled its bucket up with a load of dirt and was holding it high in the air heading towards Wayne. Wayne ran up the nearest dirt mound. The tractor started plunging into it taking dirt away as it went. The earth shaking thuds as the tractor strikes shakes Wayne, and makes him lose his balance. His mind wanders back to the time when he was young and playing king of the mountains. Wayne looks behind him and sees the back hoe reaching its long arm up trying to get him. The tractor plunges once again into the dirt pile and Wayne is knocked back and falls towards the back hoe.

The next thing Wayne knew he was at a wake. He could see a lot of his relatives there and they all were in deep sorrow. Now he starts walking towards the coffin, it1s black and well polished. He could only see a partial face, so he continues to walk towards it. When he reaches it his eyes widen in dismay. It's himself in the coffin. Then, he is in the coffin and the lid was just closed on him. His eyes open speedily.

The coffin is then lifted and is being carried to its burial place. The air in the coffin is growing thin. Wayne is frantically pounding on the inside of the coffin. Wayne's claustrophobia is beginning to show. (he could stand in an elevator or a closet all day with no problem, but just put him in a tight situation such as a coffin and he will lose it.) The coffin has stopped moving, but Wayne is still clawing at the inside cover of the coffin Now he feels the coffin being lowered, he places his palms on the lid and tries to push it open, but to no avail. Now the sound of dirt hitting the coffin is echoing inside, like the sound of rain hitting a tin roof.

Wayne forces his whole body against the inside cover, when he feels catapulted through. He lands on his face in the middle of a vacant street. The rain is falling down and puddles begin to form around him. He brings his forearms in front of him to lift the front of his body. The water is soaking through his sleeves and his arms are feeling the cold wetness. He brings himself to his feet as he looks around at this unfamiliar place. The street lights are on to defy the darkness of the night. He starts walking not knowing where he is going.

Wayne walks over to a grassy area near the road, and then stops. Water is pouring off his face, as the rain continues to drench the area. He feels something tugging at his pant leg. He looks down, and doesn't see anything at first, but then he focuses in on a dirty hand pushing its way up from the dirt below him. Wayne bends down to get a closer look. Thoughts that someone was buried alive runs through his mind, and he wants to help them. As soon as he gets close enough the hand grabs him by the arm and pulls him down with tremendous strength. Wayne pulls away and starts running.

Wayne sees an old boarded up house at the end of the road.

he figures that he'd run towards it, and maybe stay in it until it got light. When he reaches it, he opens the door with no problem, and then he enters. While walking across the rotted floor boards, one of them gave way and his foot fell through it. He just pulls his foot out, thinks about returning outside, then continues on.

The sound of water dripping in the house is the only sound

that he could hear. The smell of mildew is throughout the house. It is dark in the house, but Wayne could still see the plaster which is soaked with the rain, is peeling from the walls and ceiling.

The wind outside starts blowing hard and the house seems to move back and forth with it. Now the house is making loud creaking noises, then loud banging noises as the timber supporting the house breaks away and falls to the floor, Wayne starts for the door when a cross-beam from the ceiling snaps and knocks Wayne to the ground.

Plaster is now all around Wayne, He looks out the boarded up window and sees the sun streaking through the openings. The wind and rain has stopped, and the house is becoming light with the coming day. Wayne feels what seems to be more plaster falling on him. He rolls around on his back to look at the ceiling. When he looks up he sees large, black, hairy tarantulas falling from a hole in the ceiling. Wayne opens his mouth to let out a scream and one falls in his mouth. He quickly turns his head and spits it out. Then he sees that there were over a hundred of them crawling all over his body. He gets up fast and bolts out the door frantically wiping his hands all over his body to get all the spiders off of his body.

Wayne runs towards a gully that has a two hundred foot drop. He stops at the edge, and decides to jump the ten feet to the other side. So he backs up and takes a running head start then jumps, but doesn't make it all the way. He grabs on to the edge and is hanging there. He looks down, noticing the strain on his arms. He just can't hold on anymore, and lets go, and then falls. Just before he hits bottom he wakes up. His eyes opened so fast that they scared Anita.

Wayne looks around and notices that he's in the hospital, and that he just had a series of nightmares. His heart is still pounding from the dreams. He settles his heart down, then calls to Tom, who was on the other side of the room.

"Yes Wayne?" Tom answers as he crosses the room.

"Tom I need you to do me a favor."

"What Wayne? Anything."

"You know where Lopez is, right"

"Yes, it's on top of Red Rock Mountain."

"Well, I want you to take Anita, and all of our family and friends that you can and make your home up there."

"But why? Everyone can't just pick up stakes and move up there!"

"Look Tom, you have to trust me!"

"But Wayne, you almost died on us, you don't have all your senses yet!"

Anita interrupted.

"Anita, have trust in me. A large battle is coming up and I don't know who the winner is going to be, and I can lose my family as a direct impact."

"Well then, I shall stay down here with you and fight. I know that I could get a lot more to help." Tom replied.

"No Tom, you have to stay with the family. If something happens to me someone will be along to deliver all of you from there sometime in the future." Wayne said while disconnecting himself from the hospital equipment.

"How are we supposed to know who will truly come to help us, and who will lead us to slaughter?" Tom asked.

"Look at my right hand." Wayne extended his right hand for both Tom and Anita to see.

"See how it's dry and crumbled, see that markings?"

"Yes, it's been that way for several years now." Tom said.

"Well, look at the right hand of the one that comes to help you. There should be a similarity there."

"Let's stop talking about your death Wayne. Just hold me like we're going to be together forever." Anita said putting her arms around Wayne.

"How can you logically go against all those people, Wayne?" Tom asked.

"I learned a little trick from that group while I was in California. Anita and Tom leave Wayne's room reluctantly. Then Wayne gets dressed in the clothes that Anita brought him.

It's one o'clock in the afternoon, when Wayne leaves the hospital.

he had to sign out against medical advice, because the doctor wouldn't stick to his promise. He didn't think that Wayne was well enough to leave the hospital. When Wayne left the hospital he went across River Street to the cemetery, and walked among the tomb stones. He felt at ease in the cemetery, there wasn't any electricity in the air like there is in a crowded condensed area. Wayne walks over to the center part of the cemetery, and does something that he has never done before: he opens himself wide open, while he spreads his arms out. A gust of wind picks up, and Wayne stands there transmitting and receiving signals throughout the graveyard.

CHAPTER IX

GATHER YOUR TROOPS AND MOUNT YOIR HORSE,
THE WAR WILL BEGIN, IN DUE COURSE.
BUT BEFORE YOU CAN FIGHT,
YOUR ARMY HAS TO BE STRONG AND TIGHT.
BEFORE YOU CAN ADVANCE,
ALL YOUR MEN HAVE TO BE IN POSITION,
OR YOU'LL TAKE A CHANCE.

With all the calls completed, except for the ones overseas, Donnavin now wait's to hear from, his groups, to find out if they are in position. The phone rings, and he picks it up.

"Master, this is Rhode Island calling and we are ready."

A smile comes to Donavan's face.

"That's fine; I'll get back to you when we're going to advance." Donnavin said then hung up.

"Donnavin, do you want me to call England now?" Delfina asks.

"Yes, it is now time for them to get things ready." Delfina gets out the number for the main branch in England. They chose Cambridge because of its nick-name for being a college town, and college students have always been the target for manipulation. The main branch will in turn notify the other centers in and around that country. Then, they in turn will notify even more countries, till they reach Russia.

Delfina dials the numbers in front of her.

"Hello, this is Lavinia at the Pennsylvania branch, and the word go is implemented."

"The word go will be implemented."

"Even Wayne Homza can't stop me now!" Donnavin exclaimed to Delfina

"How long will it take for everyone to get into position?"

"Here in the states most of the centers will be ready. Sometime before nightfall the other countries will be ready." The phone rings and Delfina answers it.

"Hello, are you sure? Okay bye." Delfina gets a serious look on her face, turns towards Donnavin.

"Wayne Homza just checked himself out of the hospital."

"Wonderful, so now I get to eliminate my main opponent."

You think that he'll come straight here?"

"No, he's not foolish; he knows that we'd be waiting for him. It is my judgment that he'll get some help and then attack. Once he attacks he'll want to move swift and hard. Where did he go when he left the hospital?"

"They said that he turned down a corridor and just disappeared."

"Who do you have watching his family?"

"On his wife is Jamie. She's pretending to be a friend in this time of crises." Delfina laughs at that,

"On his mother is Dr. Phillips, and on the rest of the family I have our people taking shifts watching,"

"Good, make contact with Jamie and get a report on where Anita is. Where she is her husband soon will be." Delfina walks over to the telephone and starts to make a couple of calls. The expression on her face turns to despair as she goes from one phone number to another. Since she didn't make contact with Jamie, she went into the bedroom to where the C.B. base station was and contacted another member that was driving around and sent him to Wayne's trailer to find Jamie.

A half hour later the phone rings and Delfina rushes to answer it. "Hello."

"Delfina, this is Alvin, I'm at Wayne Homza's trailer and it's cleaned out."

"Everything gone?"

"No, just clothing and food. It looks as though they were in a hurry, cause they left the drawers open."

"What about Jamie, do you see her anywhere?"

"No. do you want me to look in the trailers of his friends?"

"No, that won't be necessary, just wait there for a minute." Delfina concentrates on where Alvin is then mentally searches for Jamie. She then sees a mental picture of a body slumped under the trailer, then she recognizes that the body once belonged to Jamie.

"Alvin, return back to this apartment." Delfina then hung the phone up and went into the next room where Donnavin was sitting in a chair waiting for a report.

"Donnavin."

"Yes, I know have all your available units converge on all of Wayne's family. Those that they can't capture, they will kill."

Delfina didn't say a word; she just went into the bedroom and contacted all of the members that she had put into place last night, just for this occasion.

"Do you think that Wayne figured out what we were doing?" Delfina asked when she returned to the room where Donnavin was.

"Undoubtedly, he figured something out. Otherwise, he would not have sent his family away. There is no way for him to know exactly what I have planned."

"Perhaps one of his family members will be able to tell us what he knows and what he's next step will be."

Disturbing calls started coming over the C.B. radio. Calls of empty households where it looked like these people stopped their daily routine, and packed up things that they needed and left. There were vacuum cleaners in the middle of the floor. And pots on the stove where dinner was going to be made.

"How can he notify all these people in such a short amount of time?" Delfina asked to herself.

"He probably did it the same way that we notified all of those centers with just one phone call. If each person calls two people, it would be completed in no time at all."

"You're right as always. I just don't like the idea of him jumping a step ahead of us. It gets me worried,"

"He only slightly has a jump on us. We will more than make up for it. And eventually get the whole of his family, they can't run anywhere we don't have people."

Tom Brinkle called as many people he could while Anita was packing up both cars.

"Tom, I can't find Jamie."

"You're going to have to forget about her we don't have enough time as it is."

"But she was there when I needed her! How can I leave her when I could help her?"

"Anita, Wayne said that we have to leave now. To linger could mean death."

"Hold me Tom, I'm afraid," Anita walked over to Tom for needed strength.

"I know how you feel, I was beginning to feel strongly about Jamie. But, both you and I know that if Wayne tells us something that we'd better listen."

"Tell me honestly, do you think that Wayne will return to us?"

"Sure he will." Tom says with tears in his eyes. "Now let's finish what we came here for. You know I feel like Noah, trying to warn people. They just don't want to listen to me."

"Well, if you didn't try, you'd blame yourself for the rest of your life."

Tom and Anita completed the packing of the cars. Then headed down towards route 11, went south on eleven till they came to the Hunlock Greek exit and went down that road, then took a series of back roads to get to Red Rock mountain. When Tom arrives at Lopez, he thinks of it as being a modern day ghost town. Most of the shops are closed and boarded up. The streets are deserted. Tom pulls over near a small field in the center of the town, and Anita pulls right behind him. Now they wait for the other members of the family and friends to show up.

Anita looks around her at the beauty of the country. The sky is a clear blue with just a few lazy clouds hanging around. The sun heating the earth to pleasant degree. Nearby is a creek babbling by as if it had eternity in its grasps, Anita always liked to visit this area to get away from the hustle and bustle of the city. In the trailer park everyone's problem became everyone else's problem. Her thoughts return to her location, and she wonders how something dreadful could happen on a day like today. She looks up and sees a car coming towards Lopez.

"Hey I heard that there's a party going on up here!" Gail Cooper yelled as she parked her car. Tom walked up to her.

"Well then, where's the booze?" Tom replied in a joking manner. "What's up Tom?"

"I'm glad that you got my note!" Anita interrupted.

"What note? I was just driving home and the next thing I knew I was driving here. I don't even know where the hell I am."

"Wait a minute, you mean that you didn't even read the note that Anita left in your trailer." Tom asked in a worried voice.

"No, I didn't even make it home. Why what's the matter?"

"Yes Tom, what's the matter, she's here isn't she?" Anita asked, "Suppose that group comes looking for us, which they will and read that note that says that we are here?"

"Daddy took care of it!" Wayne Jr. blurted out.

"That explains everything." Anita replies.

"What is going on Tom, Anita?" Gail asks looking at the two of them.

"We're not sure, it's something big, and Wayne wanted us to make camp up here in case something goes sour." Tom stated.

"If he went through this much trouble, it would have to be something really big!" Gail remarked.

Anita sat down watching her son play with Gail's girls. How fast he was growing, she thought to herself. She glanced at the pay phone, and wondered if it worked or not. Then she seen two more cars coming down the road and noticed that they were more of Wayne's family. She had tried to call them, but they weren't home. She wondered if she should chance making a collect call from that phone booth. Just then the phone at the phone booth was ringing. She hesitated then was drawn to answer it.

"Hello." Anita said in a shaky voice.

"Anita honey, this is your mother, I'm calling to tell you that your father and I are coming up for a visit." Instantly Anita knew that Wayne had a hand in this too. Then at the same time she felt real sick in her stomach, because she knew that Wayne must be in real trouble now.

"Hey Anita, come here and listen to this!" Tom yelled over to Anita. Anita ran over to Tom's car to find out what he wanted her to listen to. When she got there he pointed to his car to his car radio.

"And to repeat the latest news break. A group of terrorists broke into a weapons arsenal and killed five guards, then stole heavy weapons. Stay tuned to this station for more updates."

"You think that has something to do with why we're up here? Anita asked.

"It could, in any case I think that we should keep an ear to the radio for more updates. Anita, you stay here to listen to the radio, and we'll go through these abandoned houses to find a place for us to stay for a while."

Throughout the day more and more friends and relatives arrive at Lopez. Most were called and warned of some upcoming danger, others were overcome by a strong urge to drive out there. They came bringing whatever they could pack in their cars, knowing deep down inside that it would be a long time before they were going to return to their home.

"Delfina! Come in here." Donnavin yelled as he was about to leave the apartment.

"Yes Donnavin?"

"I'm going to prepare for the up-coming battle. Your job will be to find Wayne Homza and inform him as to where the battle will take place."

"But he'll kill me!"

"You dare to defy me!" Donnavin yelled sending surges of pain to Delrina's groin area.

"I'm sorry master!" Donnavin released the pain.

"I'm sure you'll find a way to be next to me in this battle."

"Yes I will master." Delfina says still holding herself.

After Donnavin left Delfina went into the bedroom and picked up the .38 revolver that was sitting on a night stand, then stuck it in her pants. She walked outside in the bright sunshine and started walking while she was mentally looking for Wayne.

Delfina was walking for what seemed to be hours. Sweat rolling down the sides of her face, and her blouse was drenched. She considered taking her blouse off just to cause a commotion, but she knew that her foremost thought has to be finding Wayne. After circling several blocks she ends up on North Main Street. She looks up at a sign that says: Courtright Street, and turns then she ends up climbing a hill "Tank Hill" comes to her mind as she reaches the top. She starts to follow the path, looking around at the wooded area. Then she sees him sitting below her, meditating. She stops dead in her tracks. She closes her mind, and doesn't think another thought. She pulls the gun out of her pants, cocks the hammer back, aims it.

"It won't go off!" Wayne shouted without looking back. Wayne's voice surprised her so much, she dropped the gun.

"Come down here, sit a spell. You and I were never able to just chew the fat together." Wayne said. Delfina quickly picks the gun up, points it at Wayne, and walks closer.

"I didn't come here to kill you; I came here to give you an invitation."

"Oh yes, the invitation to my funeral. Why don't you sit down on that rock over there."

"No thank you, I just want to give you the message then leave." Then suddenly Delfina felt someone grab the hand that has the gun in it, and take the gun away from her. Then someone grabbed her other arm and forced her to sit on the rock. She looked at both arms but couldn't see anyone holding her.

"Oh, I see that you met two of my friends." Wayne said turning to face her.

"What are you going to do to me?"

"Well. I have a lot of options. I know that it would be useless to try to get any information out of you. If I started torture, you'd kill yourself, and right now you're worth more to me alive, than you are dead. And yet I need to know who is in command of your troops. So what do you think I should do?"

"I think you shall let me go, and then find out when the time comes."

"No my beauty, I can't do that. I need you safely tucked away. That would mean one less of the opposition. But don't worry my friends here will take good care of you.

"How were you able to get spirits from the other world to help you?"

"It was something I learned when I went to California. It's the same trick your buddies played on me."

"Well, I must say, you are learning quick. But, it's not going to help you, because when the day is over, you will be dead."

"Boy, you're very hostile towards me,"

"You took the life of my master; I have every right to be hostile."

"A war cannot proceed without the loss of those we count on."

"Well, I might not be there to see you die, but I'll be happy to know that I played my part."

"And I thought that you might consider coming over to my side."

"You know what, if your side had a chance of winning. I would cross over to your side."

"Well, eventually good will prevail over evil. It may not be this night, but our time will once again come to reign."

"Wayne, I could almost believe you but, I know that I will have a high place in office. And I will help to stop the good people of this nation from taking it back."

"You're forgetting one thing and that is me. Before your group can take over, I must be dead."

"Somehow I think that will be accomplished,"

Delrina's thoughts go to Wayne. She looks at him sitting there and wonders how it would have been if she decided to side with him. She sees his spirit as being a calm and gentle one, and yet she knows that is the very thing that would be the end of him. By all reasoning he should have killed her, but the fool was too sympathetic.

"Okay, where will the battle take place?" Wayne asks.

"Industrial Park in Nanticoke." Delfina says in a soft voice, with her eyes looking towards the ground.

"Well, I guess that I better start heading towards that direction Wayne says while he was getting up.

"No Wayne, you'll be killed." Delfina says grabbing his arm.

"You know as well as I do I must go."

"Join with us your power will assure us the world."

"There will be no compromise." Wayne looks down at Delfina. He notices that she actually has tears in her eyes.

"There may be some hope for this world after all." He thinks to himself, as he went to get his car.

CHAPTER X

MEN BECOME BOLD,
WARM HEARTS TURN COLD.
NATIONS TORN APART,
BECAUSE THEIR CHOICES ARE NOT FROM THE HEART.
BE PREPARED TO FIGHT,
THE WAR WILL BEGIN TONIGHT.
THE LIFE OF THE ENEMY WILL BE WORTHLESS,
BUT HE WON"T DIE PAINLESS.
FOR WE WILL STRIKE AT THE CORE,
AND WIN THIS WAR.

Wayne gets into his car and heads towards Nanticoke. He knows that they will be waiting for him; he's just got to get rid of as many of them as possible. then the rest will give up and run. He wonders who their new leader is. He thought that Delfina would be the new leader, since she was number 2 when Donnavin was alive, it would be only natural that she'd be number one now. But number one doesn't become a messenger he sends number 2 or someone else.

"Well, whoever it is, they can't be as powerful as Donnavin." Wayne thought to himself. Then he started thinking over in his mind the route that he will take.

As Wayne was thinking over the route, he kept a mental picture of the
area. Then he remembered when he and his friend Karl Drum went double dating, they went into Industrial Park to park to make out with their girlfriends. Wayne was with an old girlfriend of his, Phyllis Dombrosky. Wayne and Phyllis would have been married, but Phyllis died. He remembers telling Karl to drive because he was busy in the back seat. Karl and his girlfriend had already finished, and Karl was ready to drive. As he started to drive down the dirt road. Wayne made the comment that fornication was against the bible, and right after he made that statement the car just stopped dead.

To this day, Wayne cannot figure out why the car went dead. With all the knowledge he has obtained throughout the years, he can't figure that one out. Wayne looks down at his watch and notices that it is five o'clock. He has just entered Nanticoke and is parking his car. Now he will have to walk the rest of the way.

The people that arrived at Lopez so far started to unload their vehicles. The boarded up houses will be very crowded. Families are doubling up. After Anita unloaded her car, she sat in the room she found for herself and her son, and listened to the transistor radio. She was now waiting for the five o'clock news report.

Tom figured that he should take charge and direct the people that are arriving to possible empty houses.

"Tom! Tom listen to this!" Anita shouted as she ran out of the house she was staying in.

"'What is it Anita?" Tom asked, other people started gathering.

"Listen to this news report,"

"And in Cleveland the communist group seized a police station and is holding all occupants at gun point. In San Francisco a terrorist group blew up several commercial power stations. Miami a police station blew up in flames, the same terrorist group that broke into the arsenal claims responsibility for that. And in Texas several oil wells were blown up. No one is taking responsibility for that one yet. I swear folks, what is the world coming to. It's good to know that we have sane law abiding folks here in good old Pennsylvania."

As Wayne walked down the main street that goes through Nanticoke, he felt that there was a rifle trained at his head. Before the assailant could squeeze off a shot, Wayne drew his pistol and shot him.

Wayne looks around and notices that the town is very unusually quiet. At this time of day there are people all over the streets and cars driving up and down the street. Nobody came running when they heard the shot. Wayne starts walking through back alleys. He does not want to be out in the open.

As he walks down a narrow alley, he hears a noise behind him so he turns around quickly. In his mind he sees a person hiding behind the wall at the entrance. In his hand is a pipe. Then Wayne quickly turns back around just in time to stop a 2x4 from cracking his head open. Wayne crosses his hands and stops the board from hitting him. He then grabs the board and kicks his attacker in the groin, then in the face. Then Wayne grabs the board with his other hand, turns quickly and uses the board to block the pipe that the guy at the other end attacked him with. The guy kept on swinging the pipe at Wayne and Wayne kept on blocking it until he landed a round horse kick into the guy's chest. This caused him to fly backwards clutching his chest. When he hit the ground all of the air was knocked out of him, and he was heaving.

Wayne then throws the board down, and continues walking through the alley. When he gets to the other side he could hear a car driving on the streets in the distance. Than the car gets closer, soon it turns the heading for him. Wayne looks at the car, it's a convertible Buick, supped up. Driving it was a woman. Wayne takes a second look, and the woman was naked. After she seen him looking at her body, she aimed the car for him. Wayne waited till she got right up to him, then leaped, rolled onto the car back first, then rolled off landing on his feet gun drawn. The girl did a donut then aimed the car at him once more. Wayne aimed at the front tires, one by one shooting holes into them. But this didn't defray the girl she kept coming with the flat tires, so Wayne aimed at her head and shot her. Then he got out of the way as the car crashed into a parked car.

Now Wayne removes the clip from his gun and replaces the

bullets that he has already shot off. Then he takes another clip from his pocket, matches the bottom of it to the bottom of the other one, then with tape that he had in his pocket he tapes the two together and replaces it into his gun.

Wayne could now see the dirt mounds that surround the industrial park. He was sure those waiting there heard the shots that he fired. So he decided that he will work his way up to one of the hills. Wayne runs from one barricade to another, until he finally reaches the hill. He started ascending the hill, mentally looking at the top, but not seeing anything. The hill was very slippery and hard to climb. Just when Wayne was able to see the top, his senses told him to look beneath him. He looked quickly and saw six men running toward the base of the hill with guns. When the men saw Wayne look around, they stopped running and started firing. Wayne grew angry fast, created incendiary fire. The men and their weapons were all charred,

"Damn, I didn't want to do that!" Wayne yelled to himself.

Wayne reached the top of the hill to find a gully at the other end. He still had a way to travel, before he would meet head on with the group leader. Ho descends the hill and starts walking down the gully. He hears a motorcycle behind him or maybe it's in front of him. He can't tell the noise is vibrating the hills. Then he turns around and in the distance could see a dust cloud. Then he looks in front of him and sees another dust cloud. He moves to a straightway part of the gully, and waits for the one that's in front of him. It's coming into view now, he could see the bike and the rider, then he sees a shot gun mounted on the handle bars. He freezes in his spot, staring at the bike in front of him. Then just before the rider squeezes the trigger, Wayne drops to the ground. The scatter shot hits the bike rider behind Wayne. Wayne rolls over and waits for the bike to drive by then gets up with gun drawn. By this time the motorcyclist was ready to make another pass. Wayne aimed for his chest then shot twice, knocking the rider off his bike.

Wayne started running through the gully. Just before he reaches the entrance to the small valley on the other side of the hill, he stops to glance around mentally. He has a picture of a lot of men and guns trained on all the entrances. Then he could hear footsteps snapping twigs, coming towards him from behind. He tries to mentally see what's coming, but can't. All of a sudden, the naked girl that he shot in the head comes into view. There's a streak of blood running down

142

from a small hole in her forehead. The back of her head isn't there, it's scattered all over the seat of the car. Wayne then mentally calls upon his spiritual friends; two of them stop the girl, then remove the spirit that was possessing the girl's body. When the spirit was being torn away, it let out a horrifying scream. Then before the body collapsed, the spirits caused it to walk into the entrance of the small valley.

While the girl was walking towards the entrance, Wayne climbed the hill and stationed himself on top. As soon as the girl came into view, they opened fire on her, her body was badly mutilated by the bullets thrashing through, ripping and tearing as they went. As soon as any gunman showed himself Wayne shot him. Soon all eyes turned in on Wayne's position, and they started firing at him. His high point advantage came in handy, he had a couple of them running for cover. He finished his first clip, turned it around and started on the second one.

Wayne was running out of bullets his attention was drawn to a dead man laying below him. Next to the dead man was a M—16 rifle, Wayne used his telekinetic powers to bring the gun to him. The rifle broke away from the grasp of the dead man and slowly dragged towards Wayne. Wayne was releasing his energies slowly, ignoring the bullets riddling the crest of the hill that Wayne is using for cover. As soon as the gun reaches Wayne, he chambers a round, puts his pistol in its holster, puts the M—16 on semi, and starts taking aim at the gunmen.

While Wayne was firing at the gunmen, the dead man that Wayne got the M-16 from suddenly gets on his feet and starts running towards Wayne. He then pulls a hand grenade from his belt, pulls the pin while squeezing the spoon, Wayne sees him out of the corner of his eye and turns the gun towards his direction and fires at him, but to no avail. Wayne then calls on his spirit friends, but they don't show. So Wayne concentrates on one the guy's legs, there after it explodes flying a couple of feet in front of him. The guy immediately falls, the hand grenade falls under him, then shortly after goes off insuring the guy doesn't get up again.

Wayne senses more people coming from behind him, he turns around but doesn't see anyone. He can't use the other side of the hill for cover, because he'd get shot. And yet he could feel the pressure of others aggressing towards him from behind. Wayne looks in front of him and sees more and more people completing a half circle leading up, to the hill that Wayne is using for cover. Then slowly the half circle starts to become a full circle around him he tries to shoot the new comers but someone would take their place. Within a matter of minutes the circle of people is completed around him. All of them stand up and aim their guns at Wayne.

Donnavin is waiting in west Nanticoke for the right time to join the war. He knows that it started because he could hear the gun shots, and he's keeping touch with one of his members perched in a position where he could see what's happening and relay the information by a two way radio, Donnavin could feel Wayne releasing his energies, but could tell that he is holding back. He knew that he'd have a lot of losses in this battle, but in all battles you will have heavy 'casualties.

Donnavin turns his thoughts to Delfina; He can't find her, either physically or mentally. He knows that she got the message to Wayne, because he's there, but where is she. He sent a couple of his men to go looking for her. Donnavin was hoping to combine their powers to defeat Wayne Homza. But he now realizes that he will have to do it himself,

Wayne abruptly stands up and causes intense heat to be trained on all of the guns. The people immediately drop the guns, which are hot enough to glow. Then they all charge at him up the hill, Wayne's eyes open wide, anger is seen in his face.   The earth begins to shake, the people in the middle of the hill fall, and tumble down.   They get up and run away from Wayne. Wayne sits down, crosses his legs and looks down in front of him.

There's a chill beginning to form in the air. It's 7:00 P.M. and it's starting to get dark. Wayne looks to the west and sees the sun in a far off distance. It's heat tapering off. A slight wind kicking up blowing Wayne's hair enough to let him know that he will have to be on his guard or else all is lost.

Wayne grabs the M-16 rifle, stands up, then moves to another location of the hill. He knows that the group had gone to get some more weapons, and regroup. It didn't take them too long to gather their courage and charge again after Wayne. They made the circle once again, but this time they came at him shooting, Wayne shot a couple of them, then caused a large gust of wind to arise and blind the people with clouds of dust. Then the wind got stronger and knocked them over. They once again retreated to regroup,

Donnavin felt strong energies being released, across the river in Nanticoke. He finally accomplished what he had set out to do. As he was passively observing his radio receiver caught his attention.

144

"Red leader, this is blue observer, over."

"This is red leader go ahead blue observer, over." Donnavin said into the microphone.

"We tried another charge at him but he caused the wind to repel us, over"

"Very good, have all personnel stand by. I'll be right over."

"Yes sir, I'll relay the message, over."

"By the way, were there a lot of casualties on the last charge, over."

"Minimal casualties sir, over," "Good, over and out,"

Donnavin got into his car and drove across the bridge to Nanticoke He then met with his group to tell them the next stage in his plans.

Wayne periodically looked at his watch in order to figure out how long the group is staying away. He now notices that they were away for fifteen minutes. His wait for their arrival was over. In front of him were a group of people, they were all together in one group, and didn't have any weapons. Wayne tried to figure out what trick they were trying this time, but couldn't. He sat up and crossed his legs in an Indian type of position waiting for someone to take a shot at him, but no one did. The group stopped near the base of the hill, and stared at him. The members of the group started separating, causing a path to run up the middle. Then a person walks up the middle towards the front, Wayne sees the person then stands up.

"Jeffrey Pulp! no, Donnavin!" Wayne says to himself,

"Yes Wayne Homza, it's me!" Donnavin says as he walks towards the clearing, Wayne descends the hill, and walks towards Donnavin, Donnavin stops in the middle of the clearing and faces Wayne, Wayne stops five feet from Donnavin. The group made a circle around the two.

"I should have suspected that you were back." Wayne stated.

"You couldn't, I was continually putting you off the track."

"Even so, when there are two with equal power, they should know of each other,"

"Equal! Not quite, not to sound vain, but I do have a slight edge over you. And while we're on the subject, I must congratulate you on holding back your powers. But as you see there are ways to make you use then, do you feel yourself drained yet?"

"Have no worries about Donnavin, I could still handle you with or without your cheap shots."

"That has yet to be seen. By any chance have you seen Delfina anywhere on your travels?"

"Delfina who? Oh you Mean Lavinia! If you change the name of skunk, it will still spray you with its stenchy perfume."

"So much for philosophizing, now for old time sake, where is Delfina?"

"For old time sake Donnavin, forget it! In our last battle you made some remarks about Phyllis Donbroski that I did not appreciate at all. Now your girlfriend will not be able to help you in this battle, you're going to have to rely on these derelicts."

Donnavin1s expression didn't change; he continued to stare at Wayne with a cold stare. Even though Donnavin was in another body, Wayne could see him the way he looked in his old body. Wayne remembers the deep set eyes, his forehead creating a shadow over his eyes. He was expressionless then also.

A moment of silence has past, and then the members of the group put their hands together and started humming in unison. Wayne could feel the weak energy that they were generating. Then Donnavin started drawing on the energy. Wayne looked around him, and then created a large circle of fire just in front of the group. Donnavin immediately puts it out.

"You'll find it hard to scare my derelicts!" Donnavin stated.

"If you say so." Wayne said, and then found the strongest person in the circle, concentrated, mentally saw his blood boil, then that power blew up. The group's members just closed the gap and continued humming.

"I'd be foolish to waste my energies on these people and have none left for you now wouldn't I?" Wayne asked.

"You would disappoint me if you did." Donnavin answered, and then turned his destructive power towards Wayne, Wayne immediately closed himself to all of the outside influences. The power was bringing back memories of his last battle with this man, and the fact that it almost killed him. This time Wayne feels frozen, he can't move. He then telekinetically pulls one of the members in front of him and places him between Donnavin and himself, the member starts screaming very loudly. Wayne feels the release of power from him, then does a running ace kick at Donnavin, Donnavin gets knocked back, then down to the ground. Wayne then causes the dirt to cover Donnavin in his attempts to smother him, Donnavin just barely recovering from having the wind knocked out of him causes a large gust of wind to remove the dirt from on him. When the dirt uncovers Donnavin, Wayne leaps towards him, but Donnavin sees him and causes Wayne to abruptly fly the other way. Wayne hits the ground hard, then shoulder rolls to his feet. Donnavin then tries to make Wayne explode, but Wayne mentally caused things to be tossed at him. Donnavin had to decrease his concentration to protect himself.

Wayne feels much drained now; he doesn't know how much longer that he will be able to hold out. But he knows that he has to try to get Donnavin off guard somehow or else Donnavin will win. Wayne once again charges at Donnavin. Donnavin repels him with a large amount of energy. Wayne gets knocked back into the group members. They start kicking him. Donnavin rushes up to him and concentrates all of his power on Wayne's destruction. Wayne is frozen once again. The battle with the group members drained him too much for this battle, Wayne couldn't do anything but put a force field around him. He was getting weaker and weaker by the second, and then all of a sudden everything got real bright, then black. Wayne had no thoughts or feelings just blackness.

Donnavin and the group members were too busy concentrating to notice a very large air craft hovering above them. This craft was as large as a city block. A bright flash of light came from the craft, and caused everyone below to go unconscious. Out of the back of it came a small craft the members of the craft landed then took Wayne on to the small craft, returned to the large ship then took Wayne to another compartment of the ship. They then put him in a vertical glass tube and hooked up wires to his chest, head, and closed it turning on the oxygen. Then the craft disappeared as suddenly as it appeared.

Donnavin was the first person to wake up. He looked around to see all of his members on the ground. He tried to remember what had happened; he remembered that Wayne was on the ground, and that he was ready to finish him off. He got up and walked over to the spot where Wayne was lying, and noticed that he wasn't there only a burnt spot where he was devoting all of his energies. Donnavin mentally looked around for Wayne, but his energies were nowhere to be found. He looked at his watch it read 8:00 P.M. so he came to the conclusion that he totally destroyed Wayne. Donnavin then started waking up the members that were laid out on the ground. A couple of them were dead, and most of them were blind. After he woke all who were going to awake, he looked at his watch and it still read 8:00 P.M. He went around to his member's watches and found that, they all had stopped at 8:00 P.M.

Delfina really didn't want to see Wayne go. He was a man that she had hated, ever since she first met him. But this man was so different from Donnavin, His spirit was calm and gentle, it brought out the better part of her. A part that she didn't see too often, because Donnavin brings out the evil in her. She watched the sun move towards the west, wondering how things were going. She knew that it was only a matter of time before Donnavin had Wayne worn down so that he could defeat him.

Her spiritual guards were making their presence known to her all of the time that she was sitting there. Every time she'd get up to go somewhere, they'd force her back down. Then when eight o'clock came around their presence were no longer being felt. She stood up and started walking; a single tear came from her eye because she knew that Wayne was no longer around. But she will cry no more for her enemy.

People arrived in Lopez that no one ever seen before. Anita was wondering who they were, and why they were there. But when one of them started hooking some gas generators and cutting electricity on in some of the abandoned houses, she knew that somehow Wayne sought them out and sent them there.

Some of the children were winding down by seven thirty from the hard day at play. The parents took them in their rooms and put them to bed. Wayne Jr. was one of them, so Anita stayed in the room with him. She had a radio plugged in to listen to the news. The background of the adults sitting outside talking about anything that would take their minds off of why they are really there is echoing in her mind as Anita nods off to a light sleep.

At eight o'clock Anita is startled out of her sleep. The radio was giving the eight o'clock news. She could hear the newsman talking about sightings of a U.F.O. around the area. Tears start flowing from her eyes as she stands up. She walks out to the door, and stands on the porch. She sees a small fire and a group of people sitting around it to keep warm. They all were laughing and joking until they saw Anita. They felt as though they should walk up to her. They all got up and gathered around her, even the people in the houses came out. When everyone was close enough to hear, Anita spoke. "Wayne is dead!" Anita said in a cracked voice, then broke down and cried. She ran into the house. Everyone in the crowd broke down and cried. Not only for the loss of a good friend, but because their future is uncertain now. Anita then confided in Tom that she was pregnant with Wayne's second child.

148

EPILOGUE

July, 1985. The spacecraft finally reaches its home Planet, Once Wayne was aboard, he gave them no problems. He was hooked up to machines which slowed his functions down to the bare minimum. The two years of the trip was equivalent to sixteen hours sleep,

The beings landed their craft on a special part of the planet especially made for the large ship. The tube that Wayne is in gets put on a track, and then moves off the craft and under the planet. Tubes carrying other beings from other planets have made a similar journey, they all end up in a very large laboratory that has a room for each being from each planet. In the rooms are familiar surroundings from that planet. They unhook Wayne from the machines, and let him wake up to observe him.

The times were hard when they first started out in the summer of 1983. Getting food and supplies were getting increasingly harder as the time went on. The United States was plagued with massive riots and everything became totally disorderly. The government would limit their assistance to overseas. It wasn't hard to pay off the Security Policemen of the Air Force to give information about how to get Nuclear Weapons and cripple their deployment.

In 1984, the Middle East countries joined together, cut off shipments of oil to the rest of the world, and then started plunging west. The people of Lopez closely listened to the news and they knew that they would have to pull all of their resources together and apply them towards survival. They started planting their own food and raising their own animals. 1985 they started building survival units underground when the fallout from the use of nuclear weapons in different parts of the world was getting dangerously close to where they were staying. Then they found out that by simulating the sunlight underground, that they could grow food down there. So they started farms underground in addition to the ones above ground.

Once in awhile a few persons would wander into their hometown from somewhere outside the little community. The person would tell them about what is going on and how he had to escape to the mountains in order to stay alive.

In 1987 the ozone layer around the earth, disappeared for a brief moment. All of the radiation caused by the nuclear weapons discharging eroded the ozone, causing a worldwide draught. The people of Lopez just went underground and lived off of the food that they were growing under there.

Wayne Homza Jr. will be celebrating his sixth birthday on the 13th of November, this is in two days. It is very hard for him to stay in his underground home, so he decides to go above ground and walk around. He looks at what once was a very beautiful place. The trees and flowers and grass are all dead. Out of them all, Wayne Jr. has felt the most pressure. All the people are looking towards him to free them from their underground life. His sister (Athena) who was born in March 1984 does not show any ability to do anything supernaturally. Wayne Jr. tries to talk to her, but she isn't very responsive to him, or anyone else. But still the two of them are very close.

Wayne Jr. heard on the news that Canada had fallen to Russia. When the news came over the radio, everyone turned to look at him. Hours have passed by as Wayne Jr. just walks and thinks. It's his way to release some of the pressures. The area that he is now in is unrecognizable to him. Its midday in November and 90. He realizes that he has to start walking back towards his home; he turns around but bumps into a woman. He feels something inside that he has never felt before.

"Hello little Wayne, how are you doing today?"

"How do you know my name?"

"Why I was a friend of your father's,"

"Lavinia!"

"Very good Wayne." Lavinia answered as she grabbed his hand.

"No, you're bad, let me go!" Wayne Jr. said as he tried mentally and physically to get away from the woman.

"Well, you're not that good." Lavinia said while applying her own power. She was able to subdue him and take him along with her.

When she arrives at Donavan's place, they both grab the child and take him to the basement. Down there, Donnavin picks up a plastic halo looking object that has pins sticking through it all around the center. And he puts it on Wayne Jr's head. Wayne Jr. immediately collapses.

"Very good Lavinia, how did you find him?"

"I was walking around in Kingston and I felt him so I went to see where he was, and here he is."

"What were you able to get from his mind?"

"Nothing, somehow he's able to keep it closed."

"I just tried also, but didn't get anything. At last now I won't have to worry about him growing up coming at me. With this machine I will be able to use his powers for my gains, by stimulating the different sections of his brain, he will do and say anything I want him to."

"How are we doing in Canada?"

"No opposition left. Alaska is about ready to fall, and then we enter the US with force, within two more years, Pennsylvania will be yours to command,"

THE END